The Doom of Ravenswood

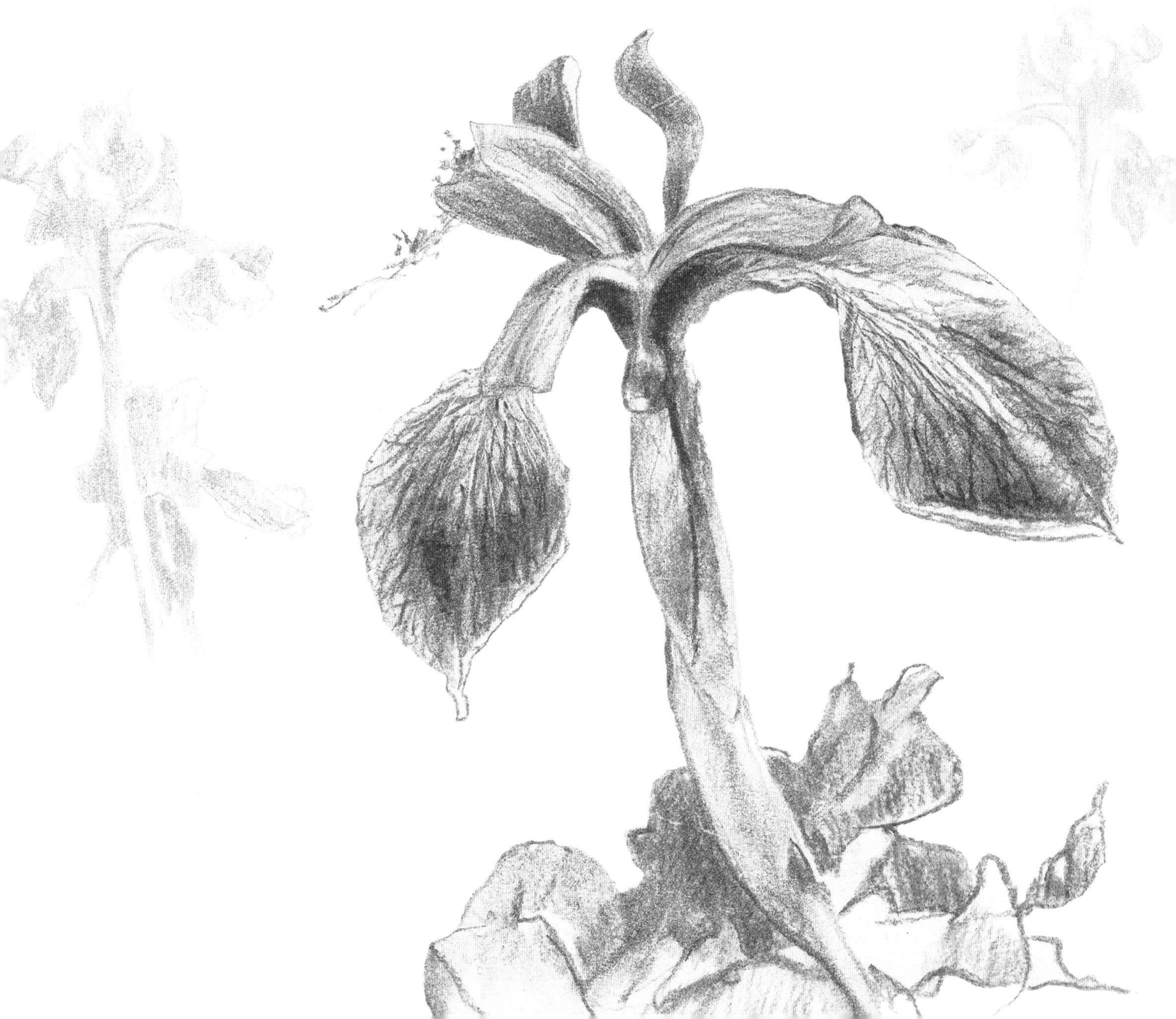

The Doom of Raveswood

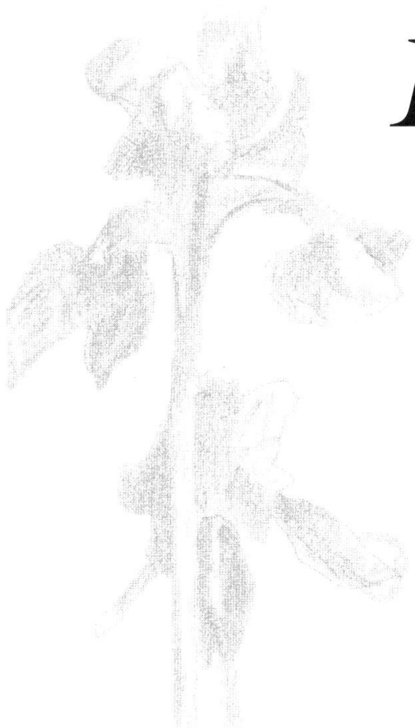

ARCHIBALD RUTLEDGE

Introduction by Jim Casada

Afterword by Charles W. Waring III

Illustrations by Stephen Chesley

THE UNIVERSITY OF SOUTH CAROLINA PRESS

A Project of the Humanities Council[SC]

Published by the University of South Carolina Press
Columbia, South Carolina 29208

www.sc.edu/uscpress

Manufactured in the United States of America

24 23 22 21 20 19 18 17 16 15
10 9 8 7 6 5 4 3 2 1

Library of Congress Cataloging-in-Publication Data
can be found at http://catalog.loc.gov.

ISBN: 978-1-61117-570-7 (cloth)
ISBN: 978-1-61117-571-4 (leather)
ISBN: 978-1-61117-599-8 (ebook)

Contents

Introduction

Jim Casada

Archibald Hamilton Rutledge (1883–1973) quite possibly ranks as South Carolina's most prolific literary figure ever. Even more impressive than the scores of books, hundreds of articles, and thousands of poems he published is the diversity of his literary output. He was South Carolina's first poet laureate, a post he held for upwards of three decades. Supposedly on not one but two occasions he was the runner-up for the Nobel Prize in Literature. As a hunting writer, "Old Flintlock," as Rutledge was fondly known to family and friends, was incredibly prolific, with nationally recognized expertise on the quest for white-tailed deer, wild turkeys, grouse, and other species. His nature writings garnered him the prestigious John Burroughs Medal. Short inspirational books with comforting titles such as *Beauty in the Heart, Life's Extras,* and *Peace in the Heart* lightened the days and brightened the ways of hundreds of thousands of readers. Poetry ranging from exquisitely constructed sonnets to free verse which flows with the silky smoothness of

Rutledge's beloved Santee River graced the pages of major national magazines on almost a monthly basis.

For the man's fans, and legions of them remain today a full four decades-plus after his death, his efforts in all these literary genres are well known. Yet one salient aspect of Rutledge's endeavors, the one which in many senses brought him to the attention of editors on a national level and began to put welcome funds in his bank account, has largely been forgotten. This is his production in the field which might be described as children's literature.

To be sure, what readers in the first third of the last century considered appropriate and engaging material for youngsters differs dramatically from that of today's world. Most, if not all, of what Rutledge wrote for youthful audiences would now be considered "over their heads," of little interest, or possibly inappropriate. In the latter context he regularly wrote stirring adventure tales on what he liked to describe as chimeras (a word which in all likelihood not one in a hundred contemporary adolescents would recognize). They involved gigantic versions of diamondback rattlesnakes, sharks, alligators, wild hogs, cottonmouth water moccasins, and other dangerous creatures of the wild. While his chimera stories were fictional in nature, they had a solid underpinning of factual information. Without exception they involved beasts with which Rutledge was intimately familiar and which he had encountered, as boy and man, on his beloved Hampton Plantation near McClellanville, South Carolina.

In terms of both quantity and quality, all of his contributions to children's literature are impressive. It might also be noted that his work figured prominently in the readers and anthologies which were in commonplace usage in classrooms during the first half of the last century. Among the magazines to which he contributed were *American Boy, Black Cat, Boys' Magazine, Boys' Own Magazine, Classmate, Haversack, Ideal Youth, Open Road for Boys, Target,* and *Youth's Companion*—a partial listing at best.

Rutledge's writings in this field have been largely overlooked by posterity, often dismissed as being of little interest, at least for adult audiences, simply because they were originally written for juveniles. Book publishers are also culpable in this regard. Most of Rutledge's book-length works of prose are anthologies comprising chapters which originally appeared in magazines. With a few notable exceptions his chimera stories are missing from these books, and to my knowledge about the only use of these tales since Rutledge's death has been the reprinting of a couple of them in the popular outdoor magazine, *Sporting Classics.* Interestingly, this publication is considered to be top drawer, a magazine geared specifically for the thinking, well-educated outdoorsman. One has to wonder how many of its readers, as they enjoyed tales such as "Death in the Moonlight" or "The Spectre of Tiger Creek," realized the material was originally intended for youngsters.

Rutledge must also shoulder some of the blame for the ephemeral nature of his writings for juveniles. With one noteworthy exception, there is little indication that he made much effort to incorporate them in books. That exception focuses on one of his earliest books, *Old Plantation Days.* Or, to be more precise, on two books bearing that same title.

Although no date of publication is given, it seems almost certain that the first rendition of *Old Plantation Days* was that from the Eddy Press Corporation of Cumberland, Maryland, about fifty miles south of the boarding school where he taught English for many years. It comprises 160 pages and eighteen stories, and I have been able to locate thirteen of them as they appeared in magazines. All of these were published between 1908 and 1911, and all but one in magazines for adolescents. That suggests that the Eddy Press version likely was published in 1912 or 1913, and it probably involved the same basic approach Rutledge used for some of his earlier books such as *Under the Pines and Other Poems* (1906), *Plantation Song* (1908), and *The Banners of the Coast* (1908). It is worth noting that *Under the Pines* also bears the Eddy Press imprint, a fact which pretty well puts paid to the suggestion of some Rutledge students that *Old Plantation Days* as published by that printer was pirated. Another circumstance arguing against the book having been published without the author's knowledge or permission is the fact that there are copies of the Eddy edition bearing Rutledge's signature, dated Christmas 1913.

My personal view is that Rutledge underwrote its publication as a privately printed item or what was in those days sometimes known as a vanity publication. Whatever the precise nature of the Eddy edition's origins, it differs appreciably from the more common 1921 edition published by Frederick A. Stokes Company, an edition still available to this day. The two books share thirteen stories in common. The Eddy Press edition has five stories which are unique to it. Similarly, the Stokes edition has fourteen new stories. The Eddy Press version is extremely rare and was likely printed in an edition of no more than 200 to 250 copies. I personally have seen only three copies of the Eddy edition in a lifetime of reading and collecting Rutledgeiana, and the paucity of listings in *The National Union Catalog of Pre-1956 Imprints,* not to mention on internet sources, is suggestive. A check of listings on the latter found a single copy—at a whopping $5,000 plus—on offer. That may be a bit higher than the work's retail value, but unquestionably the book is extremely rare.

As a result, the five tales found in it which do not appear in the 1921 edition—"The Egret's Plumes," "Claws," "The Ocean's Menace," "The Heart of Regal," and "The Doom of Ravenswood"—are unfamiliar to virtually all lovers of Rutledge's writings. Therein lies the genesis of this project, published in partnership between the Humanities Council[SC] and the University of South Carolina Press. Bringing these tales back into print provides today's readers a chance to enjoy forgotten tales from Old Flintlock, to sample and savor his work as an author of juvenile literature, and to garner eye-opening exposure to how much material aimed at an adolescent audience has changed over the passage of a century.

Changes in the nature of reading tastes notwithstanding, there is timelessness in Rutledge's writing, a quality of literary appeal, which makes these stories enduring and endearing. They are as interesting and intriguing as they were when originally published. The pieces reveal a young author in the making, and in them we see ample evidence of the characteristics which would be salient ones throughout Rutledge's career—comfortable intimacy with his subject, rare understanding of the natural world, an enviable mastery of words, and the unerring feel of a masterful storyteller. Like virtually everything Rutledge wrote, these tales of forgotten days and vanished ways belong to the ages.

FACING: "Porch, Oak," charcoal on paper, 9.5 in. x 12 in. The Washington Oak as viewed approaching Hampton Plantation, Archibald Rutledge's family home in McClellanville, South Carolina. Plein-air, 1:08 P.M., Wednesday, August 2, 2014.

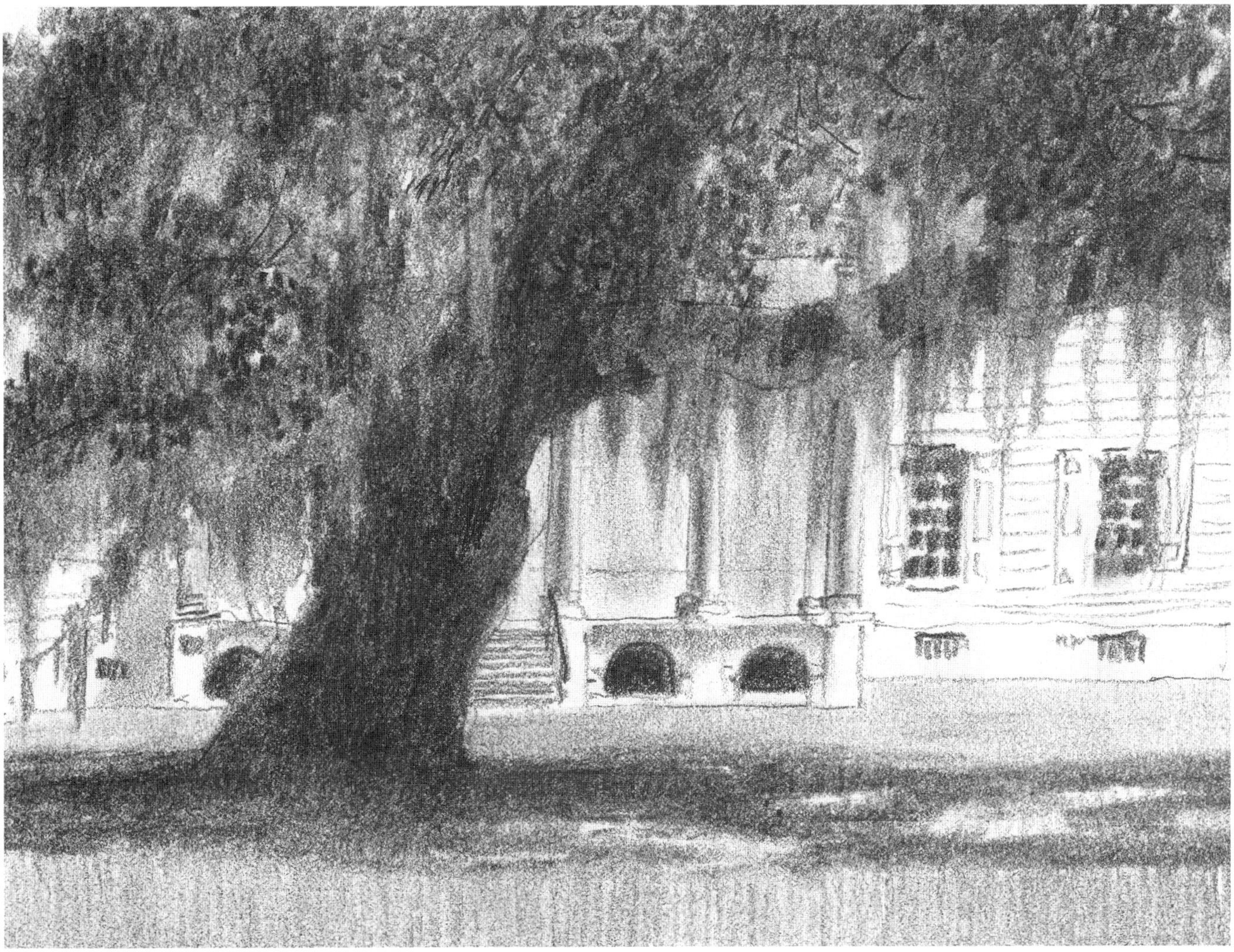

The Doom of Ravenswood

I TOOK THE LONGER AND MORE unfrequented of the two roads because the ride home to Ravenswood Plantation through the summer afternoon was delightful. Never had the woods seemed so friendly, the flowers so bright, the birds so songful. At one place the road dipped into a cool hollow, where a slow stream ran, and the underbrush rioted densely. The swamp, I knew, went by the fanciful name of the Doom of Ravenswood; though I confess that it never impressed me with any sense of impending disaster. It seemed a place full of ancient solitude, a haunt of ancient peace.

The wild blue flags were so beautiful, growing there just beyond the little white sandbar in the swampy stream, that I let the lines fall on Redbird's neck and dismounted. He immediately took advantage of my apparent aberration and began to graze on the rank and luscious grass that lined the shadowy road.

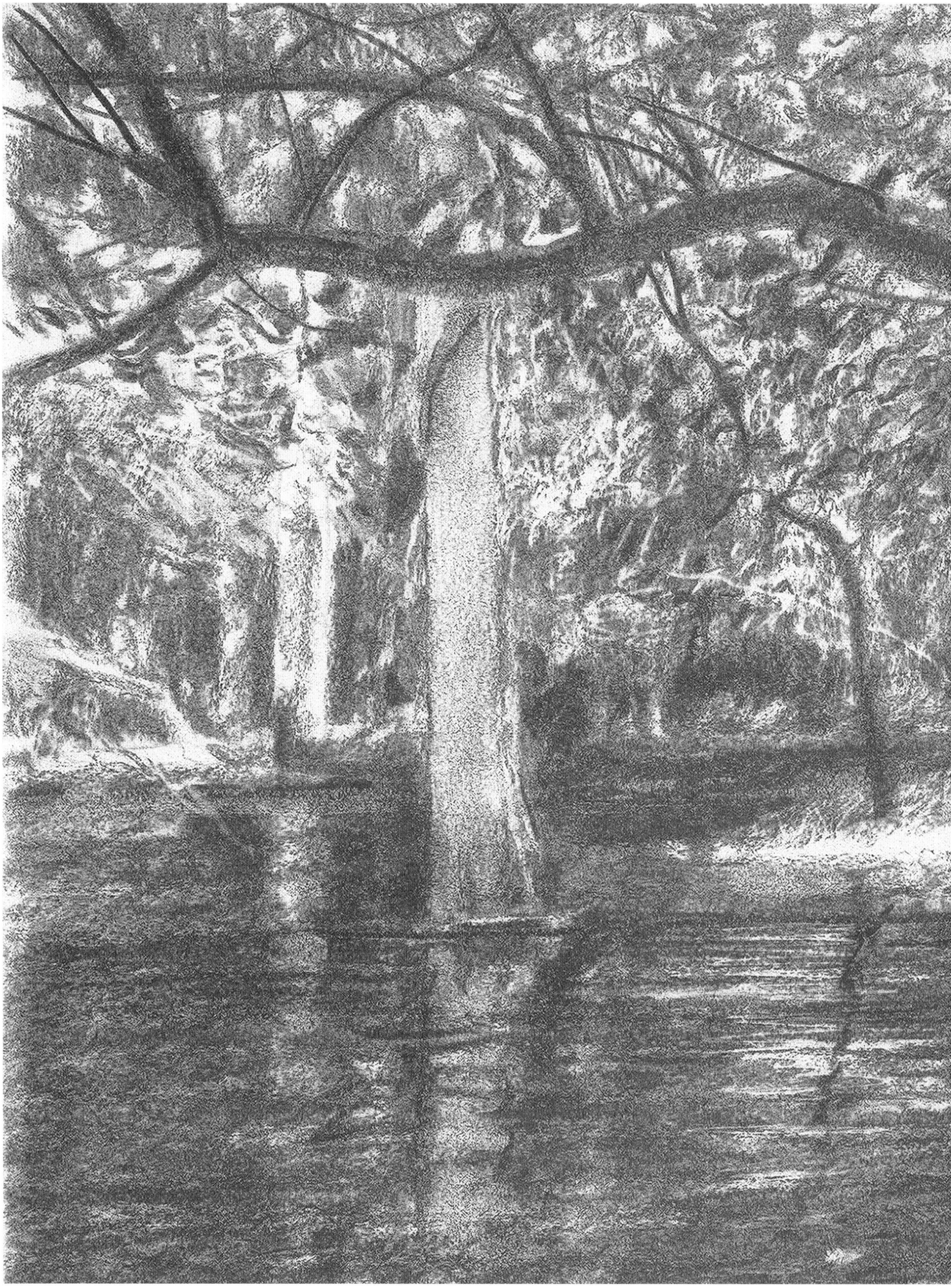

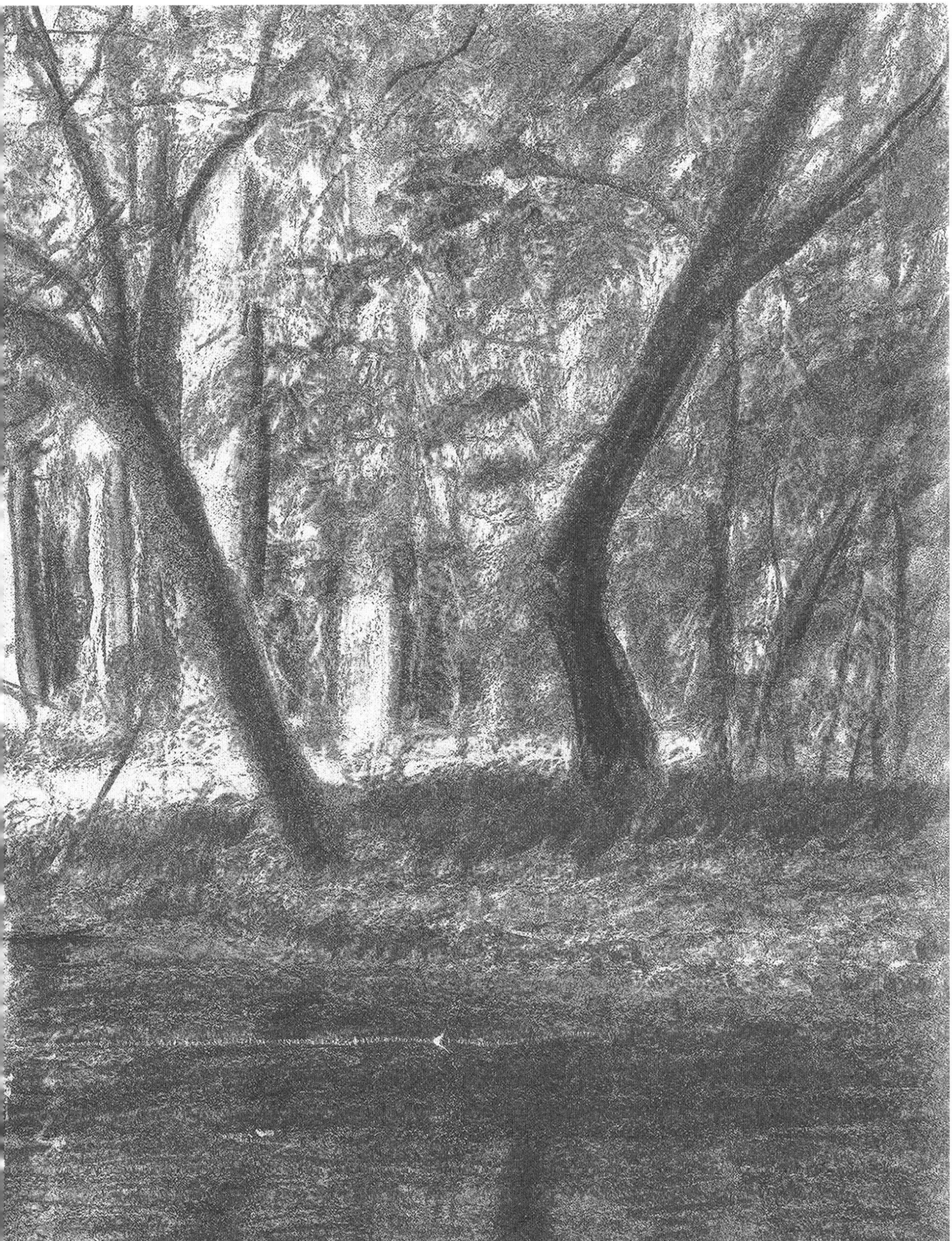

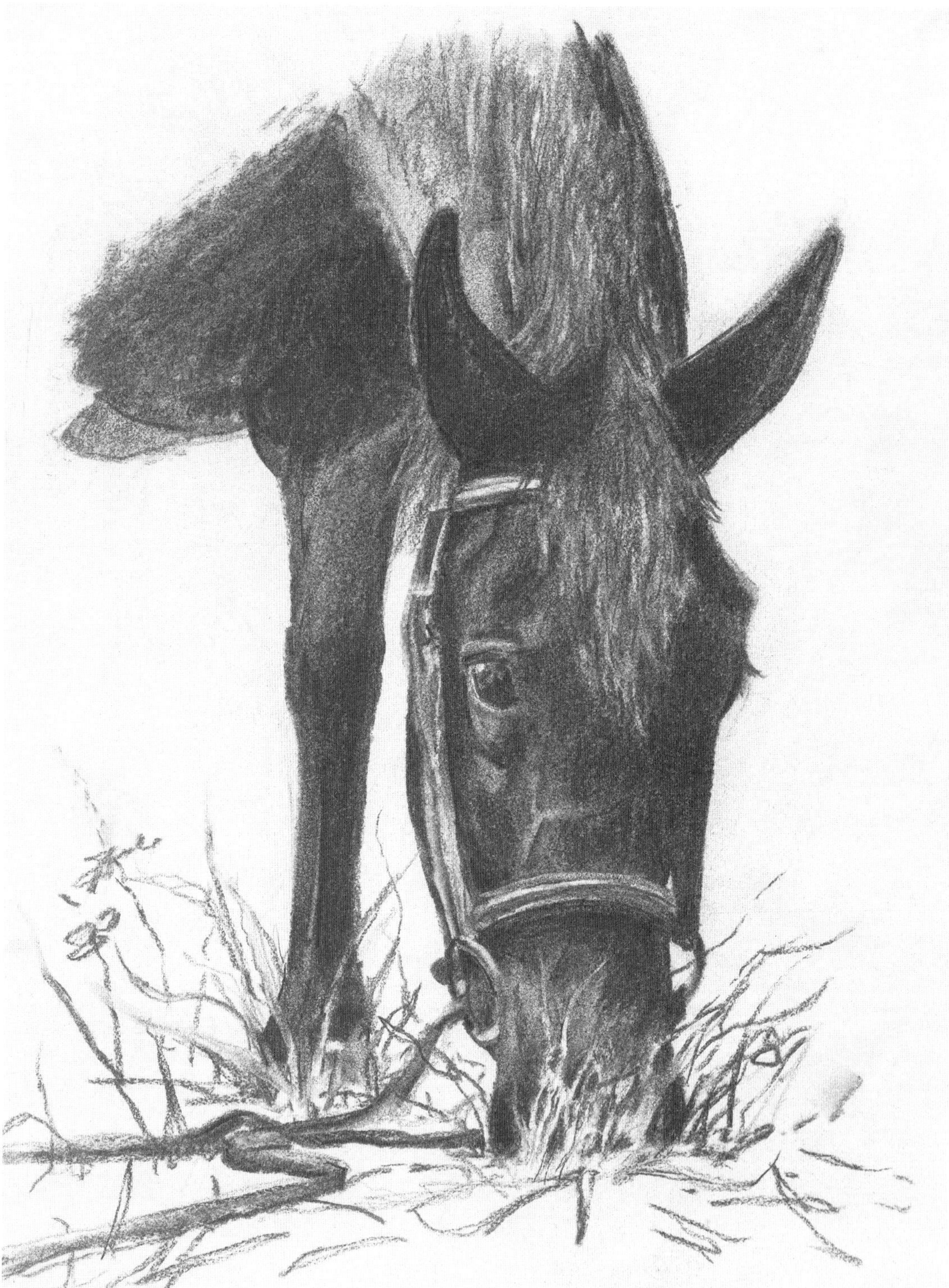

I walked out on the tiny peninsula, bending under the feathery willow boughs; and leaning down I grasped the stem of a royal flag-flower. It broke at the joint and slid out of its tight socket easily, a silver moisture dewing its stalk. I took a step farther, toward another beauty that reared its purple head just beyond my reach. I leaned far out, and my feet sank in the sweating sands; I grasped a willow limb and bent forward. Though I could feel that my feet were almost soaked through, I had made up my mind to capture that flower at all hazards. Another step I ventured; and now I was on the verge of where the black waters of the morass lipped sluggishly the shiny sands of the shore. The flag was easily within reach; strangely enough, it seemed to come nearer to me. I released the bough, which sprang back into its place. I grasped the luring flower, and as I tugged gently at it I felt myself sink. To my amazement I was over my ankles in the sucking sand. But I nevertheless pulled the flag; then I sought to withdraw one foot. I felt the other give way; I struggled, I floundered, I sank up to my knees. Then, trembling, I stood still—if, indeed, it might be called standing—for the black water had begun to bubble thickly about my legs, and they, like dead weights, sank slowly downward.

I tossed the flowers far up on the shore, noticing at the same time that my tracks had been obliterated by the watery, treacherous sand. Very gently then I pulled off my coat and laid it on the edge of the bog. If I could get my feet on it, or my knees, it might give me support until I could spring to firm ground. I put my hands on the coat, lightening the weight on my legs; but the attempt was disastrous. Swiftly and ruthlessly the whole bottom seemed to give way under my feet, and I was drawn by the monster down, down, down!

A cry and then a groan of mortal fear and agony escaped my lips; and Redbird, feeding near, threw up his head and looked at me strangely. I do not doubt that I returned his look in a way that justified his alarm. He looked startled and disheveled, for his mane was over on the wrong side, and the reins had slipped over his head and were dangling. But after a moment's gaze, he decided, evidently, that while I was acting as I should not, it was my own affair; so he buried his nose again in the fragrant grass, but kept one eye cocked with an air of not wishing to miss anything.

I was now dreadfully afraid. I could not rid my mind of the name, the Doom of Ravenswood. It was plain enough what the meaning must be. And to think that I had lived on the plantation all those years and had not known it! Sometimes I wondered how I should have to die; but I had never pictured a scene like this, never!

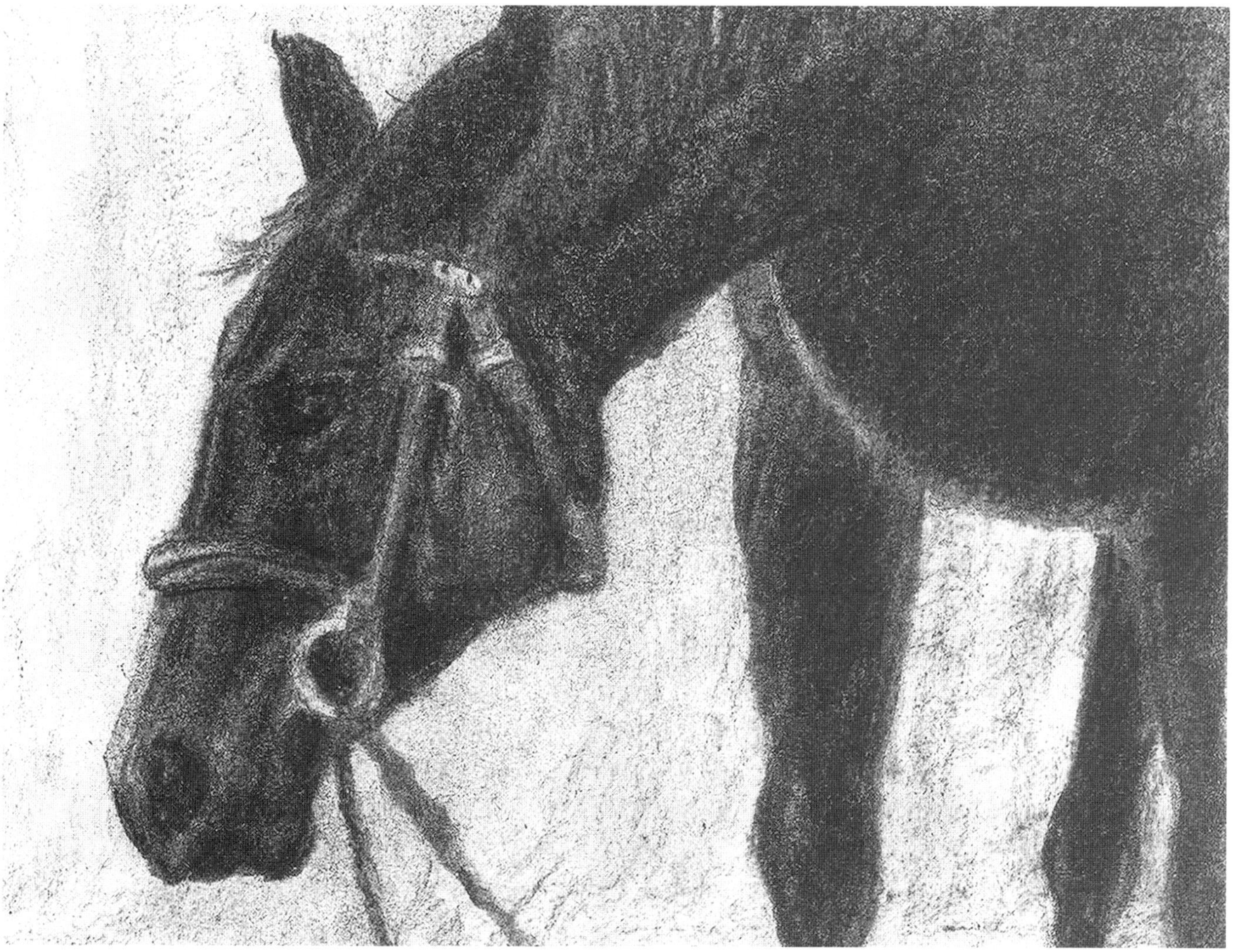

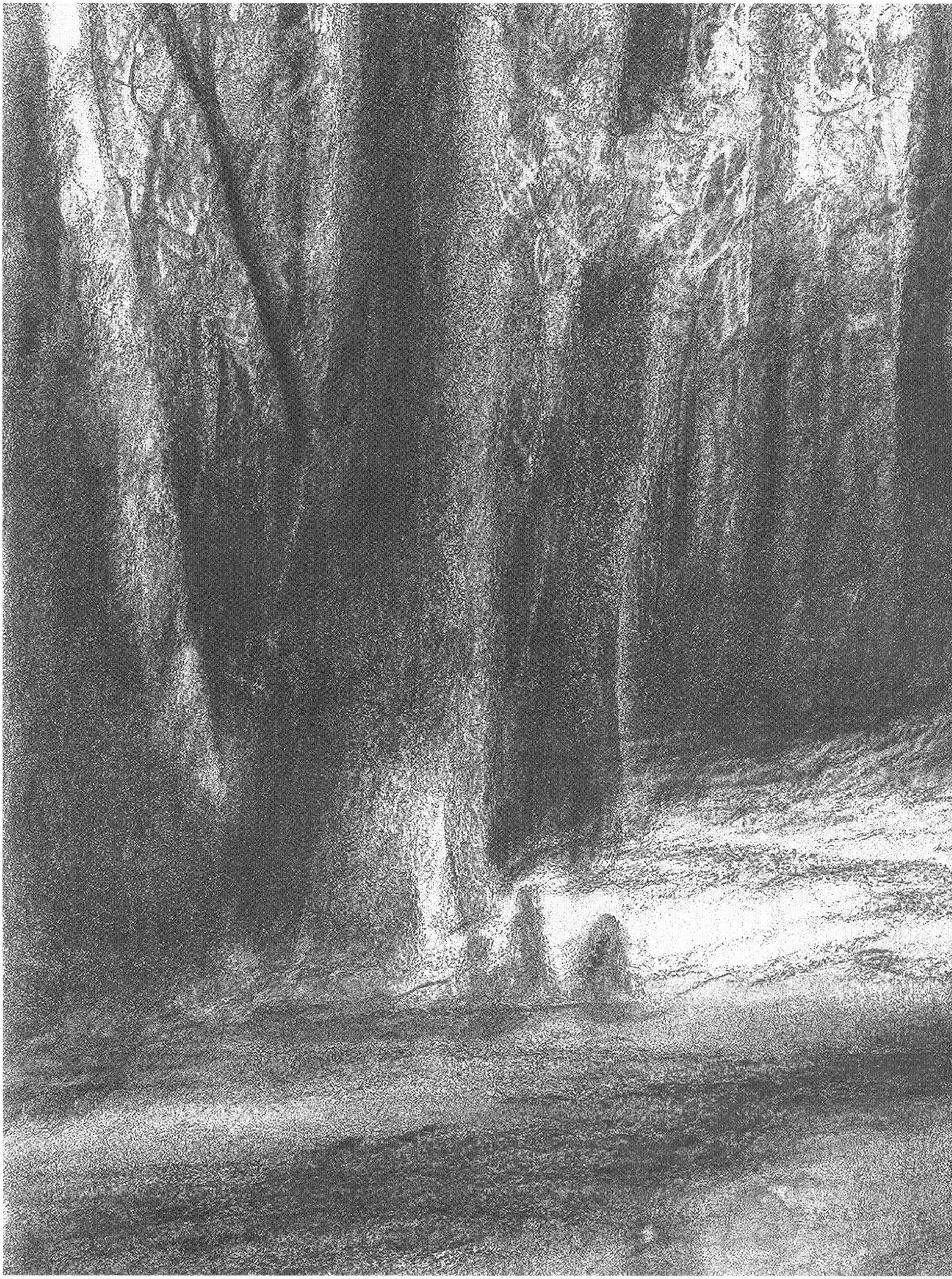

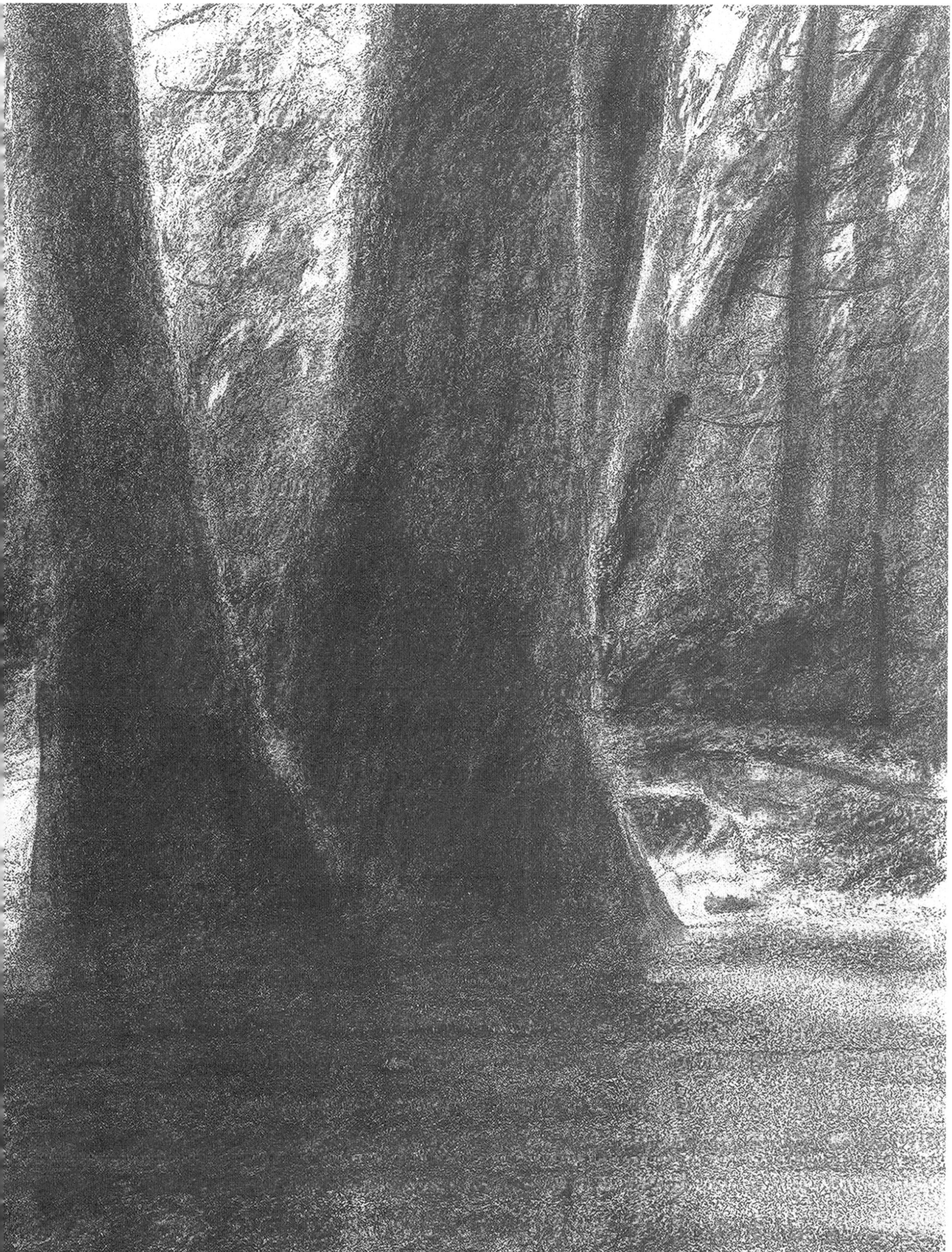

Above me were the mocking willow branches, far out of reach, and beyond them a glimpse of the happy blue sky. Behind me was the ominous morass. Before me, just near enough for the tips of my fingers to touch it, shone the little sand bank whose clean, inviting footing had lured me to my doom. Beneath me was—a sudden faintness overpowered me, and my eyes swam in dazzling darkness. The cold and gradual creeping of the water up my body filled me with nameless loathing and terror.

I must have prayed wildly, screamed madly for help, for rescue, for strength to die bravely! But it is little indeed that I remember of those dreadful moments while the sands sucked me relentlessly down. I recall that a watersnake swam near me, forcing his way cautiously through the flag stems. How I envied him his safety! He glinted at me with sharp yellow glassy eyes, then swam furtively on. A hermit thrust, sequestered far in the dewiest hear of the silence-mantled swamp, fluted a mellow song. It sounded spiritual, and as from another world. A curious blue jay dashed into a nearby bush, peered at me impertinently, scolded me softly and querulously, then flew away with glorious freedom, screaming derisively. Nature seemed to have no heart for my misfortunes, no sympathy, no help for my peril. And I had loved her so!

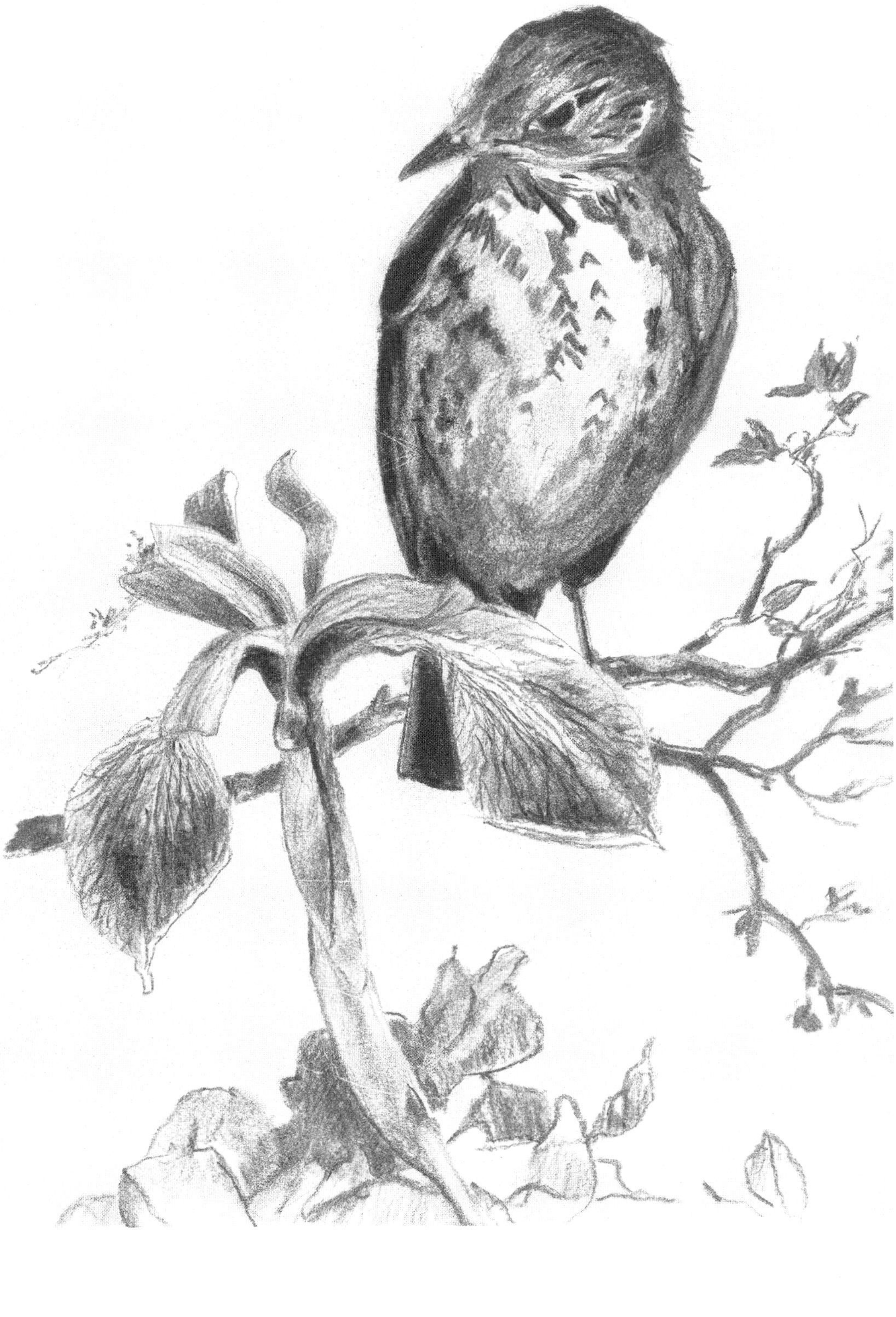

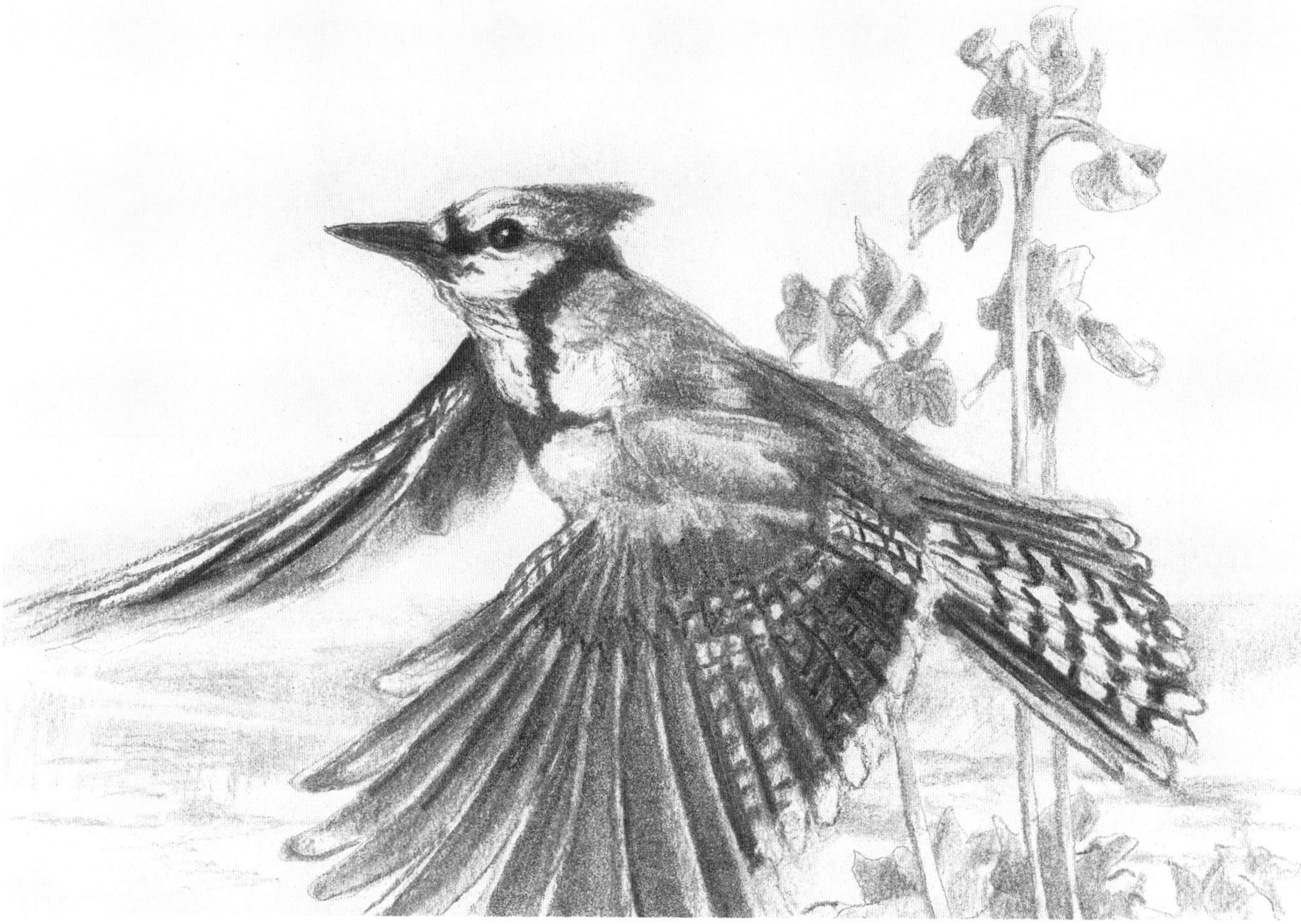

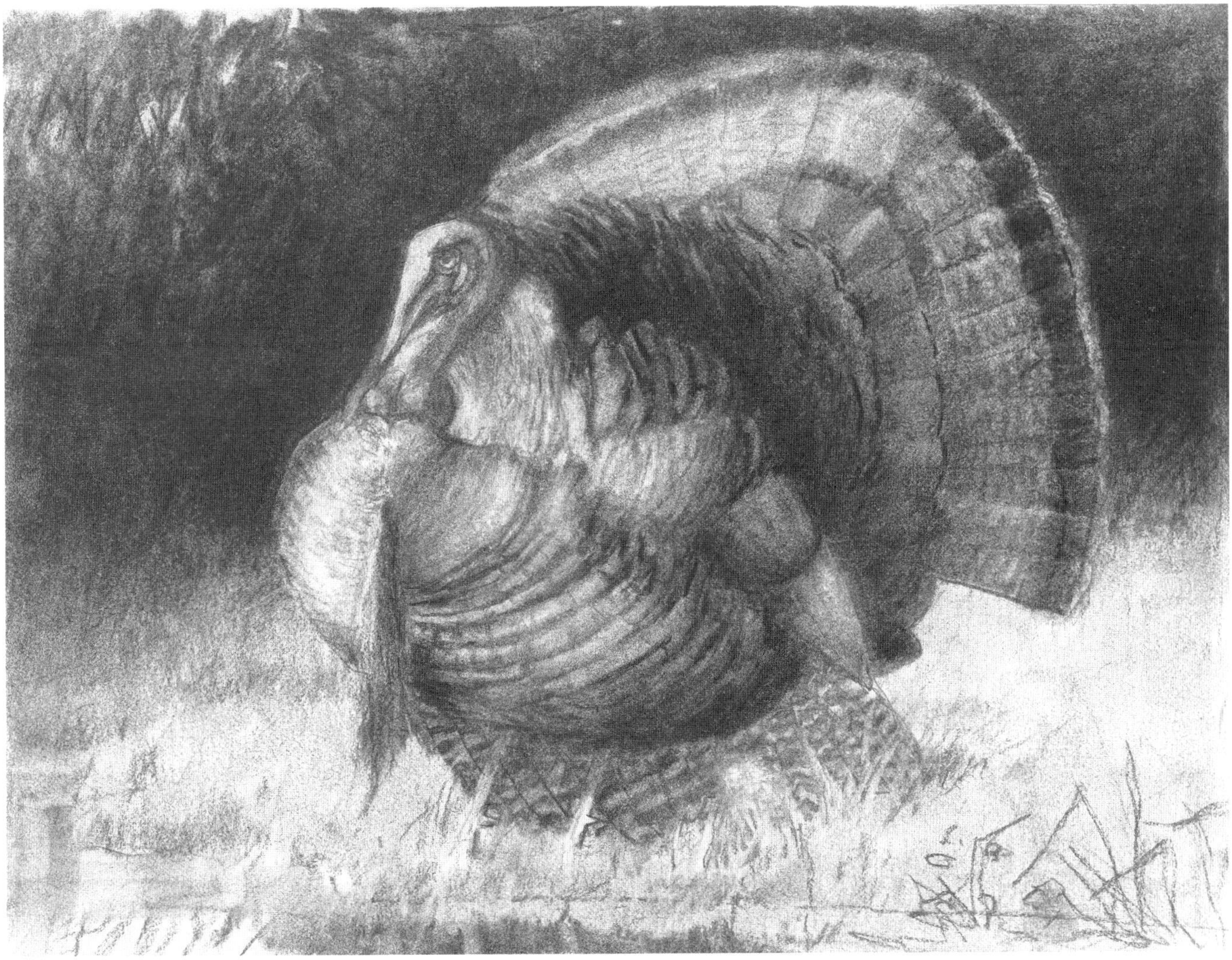

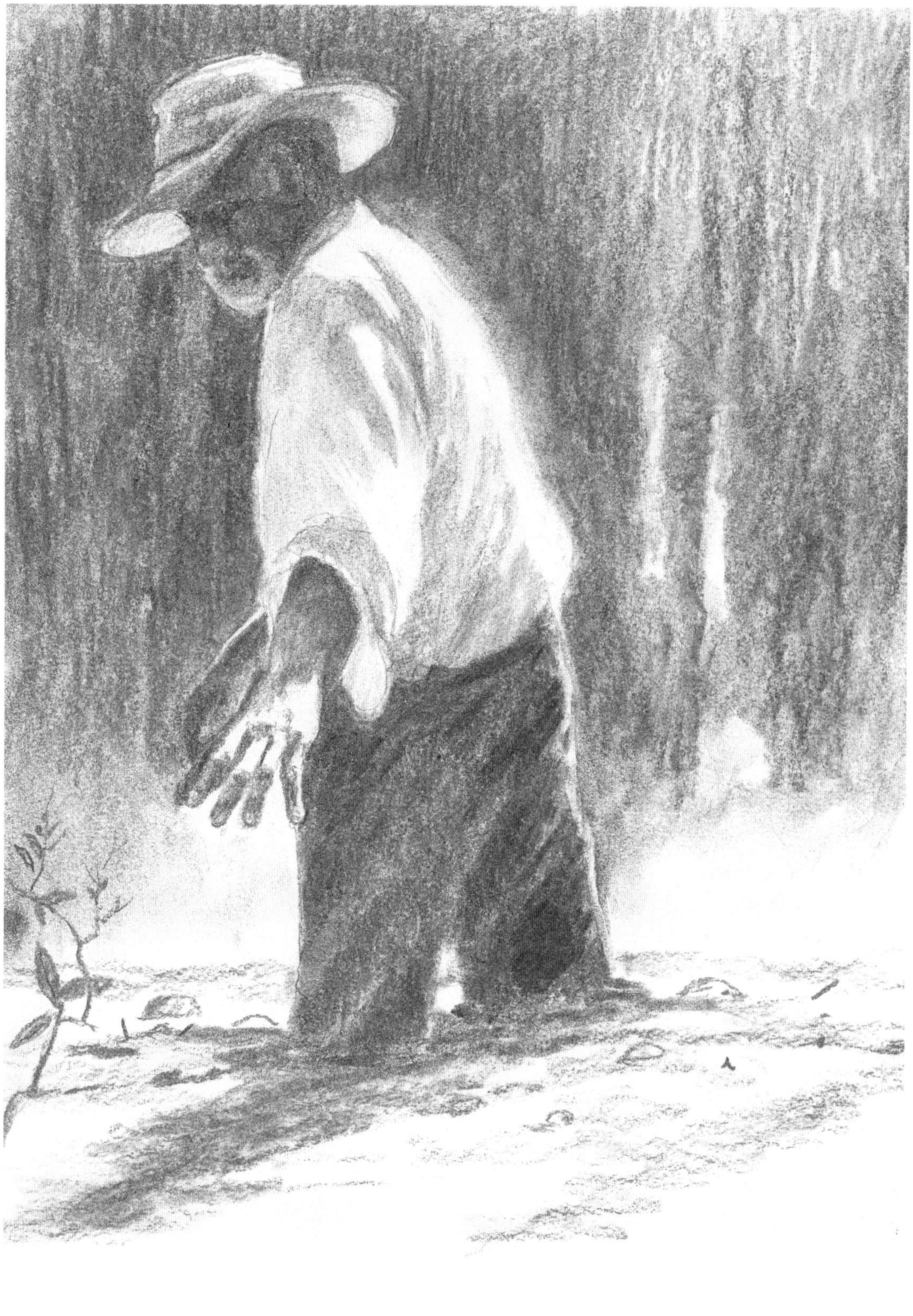

The sands were now gripping me about the waist with their sliding insidious fingers. The pressure and my fright made me breathe harder, and I grew cold through all my frame. As a boy I had always been accounted strong; and as a man my knowledge of the woods, my agility, my muscular resourcefulness were among the proudest of my personal possessions. But none of these things now availed me. Rather did they appear drawbacks; for they made me eager to struggle, where to struggle was fatal. My heart and muscles cried out for me to let them save me. But I should wait quietly, I knew, should wait quietly—Oh God! I cried, for what should I wait so quietly, so gently? What could I gain by inaction? Slowly, grimly, I was sinking in the ruthless quicksands. Mine was the Doom of Ravenswood. On that lonely road, and with the twilight falling, I could not possibly hope for a passerby to help me. My fate lay in my own hands; and wretched fate, where to put forth the strength of which I was so proud was but to sink deeper, to strangle, and to die!

With a quavering voice I called to Redbird, the horse that I loved and that loved me. I wanted to look into his eyes, to try to make him understand. If ever there was a time when he might help me, when I needed him, now was that time. I called him gently, and he whinnied his affection, lifting his head out of the deep roadside grass. In his great eyes I seemed to see a comprehending light; but it was doubtless only fear and curiosity.

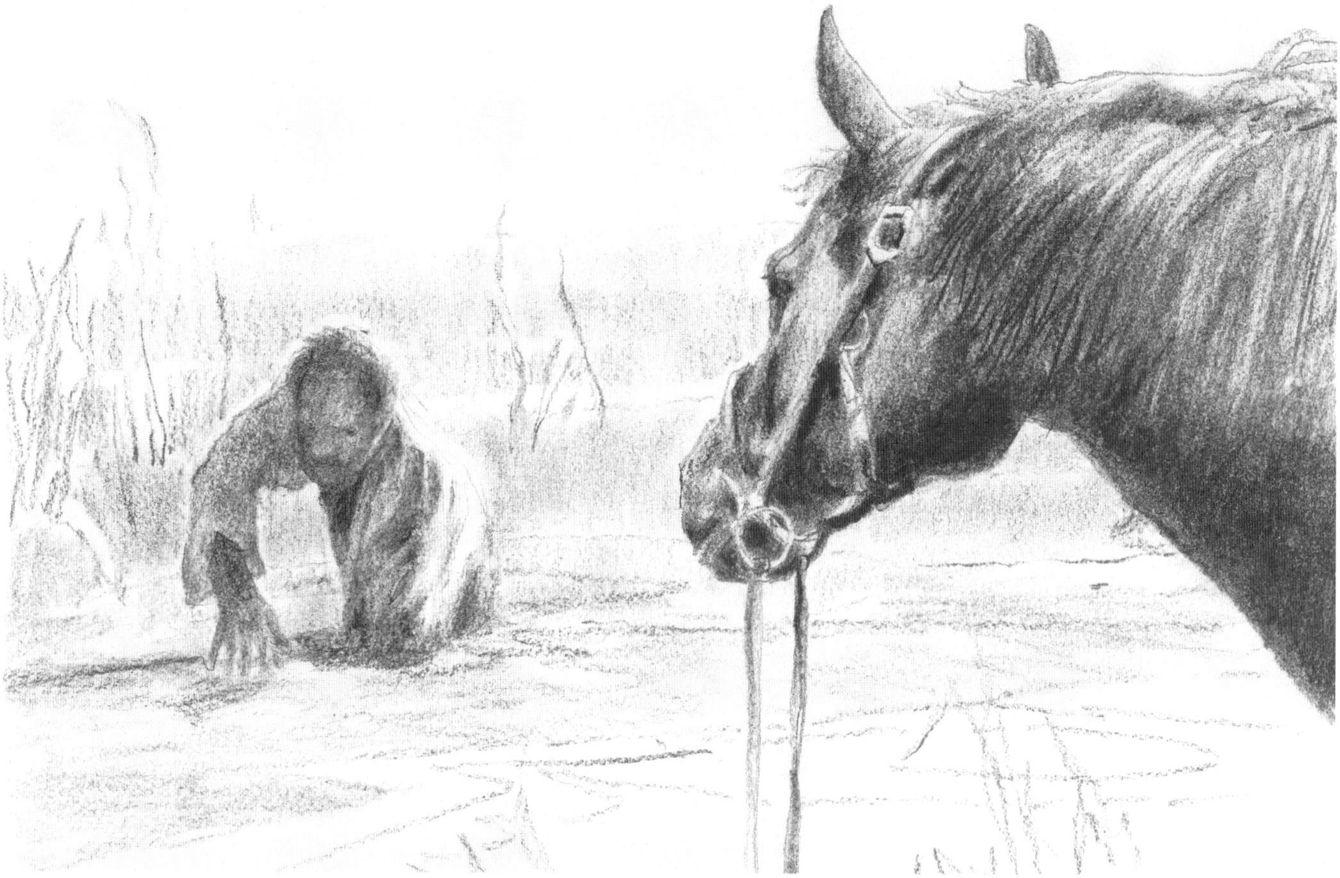

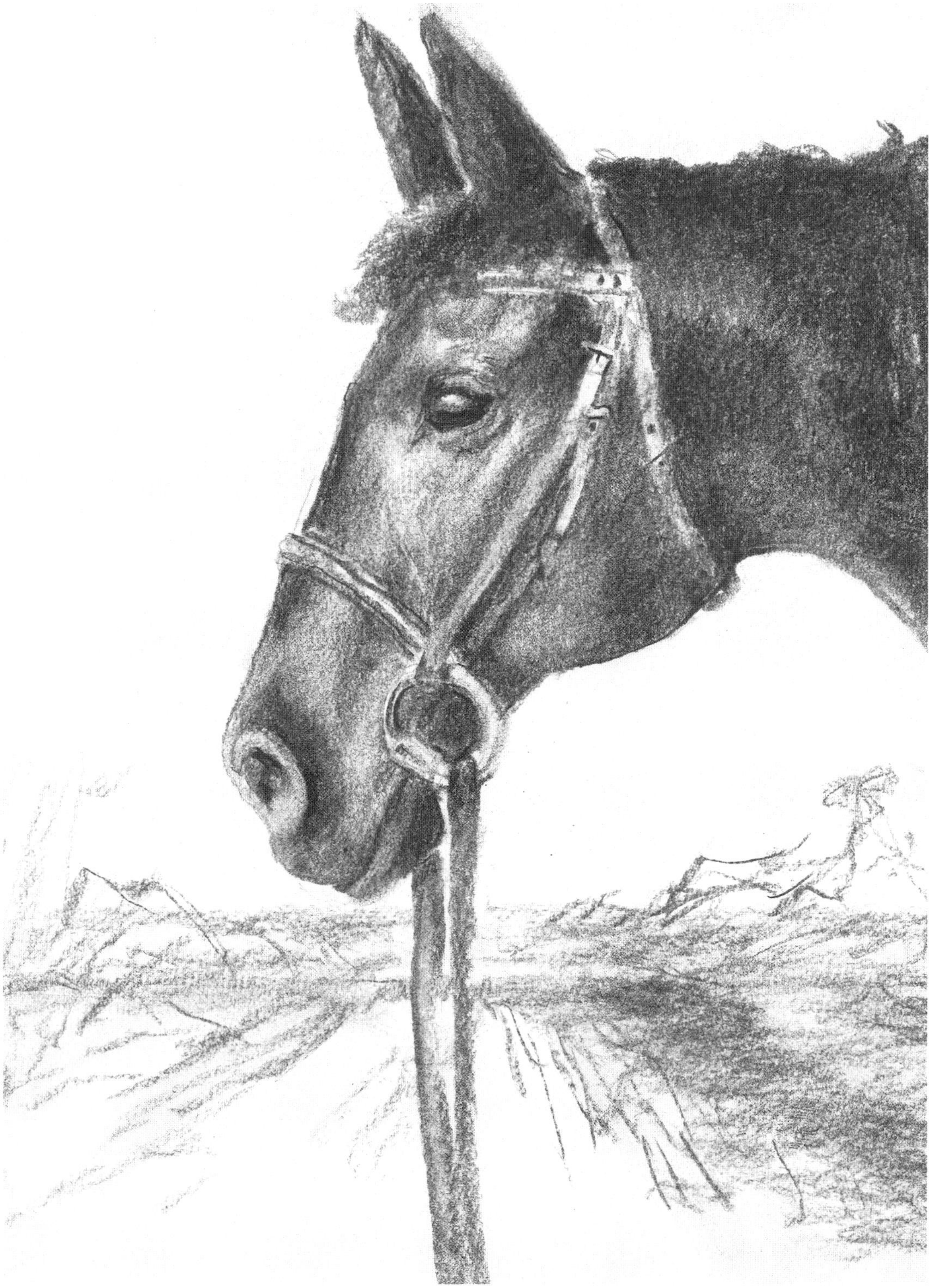

With trembling fingers I picked a pitiful little wisp of bitter sawgrass and held it entreatingly toward him. “Come, Redbird,” I said, “come, old boy.”

He gazed at me with undetermined, lustrous eyes. I felt that he did not want the grass, and I could not blame him. But he had to come! He just had to come! There was no one else to save me; and surely my Redbird would not desert me in my extremity of peril. If he would swing that loose bridle near enough to me, he might pull me out by it. But before I could reach the reins he would have to come at least part of the way on the treacherous sands. He might go down with me; or, feeling his footing giving way, he might plunge out, never to be tempted near me again.

About my breast now the tawny monster clung, seeking its prey! It was climbing up, always up. It was trying to clutch my throat, I knew. It would completely cover my chest; then my neck and chin; and then it would smother me, strangle me, drown me. And the black waters and the crawling sands would close over me silently, and close over me forever!

Running through my feverish brain were the tragic lines from Scott’s Bride of Lammermoor:

> “He shall stable his steed in the Kelpie’s flow,
> And his name shall be lost forevermore.”

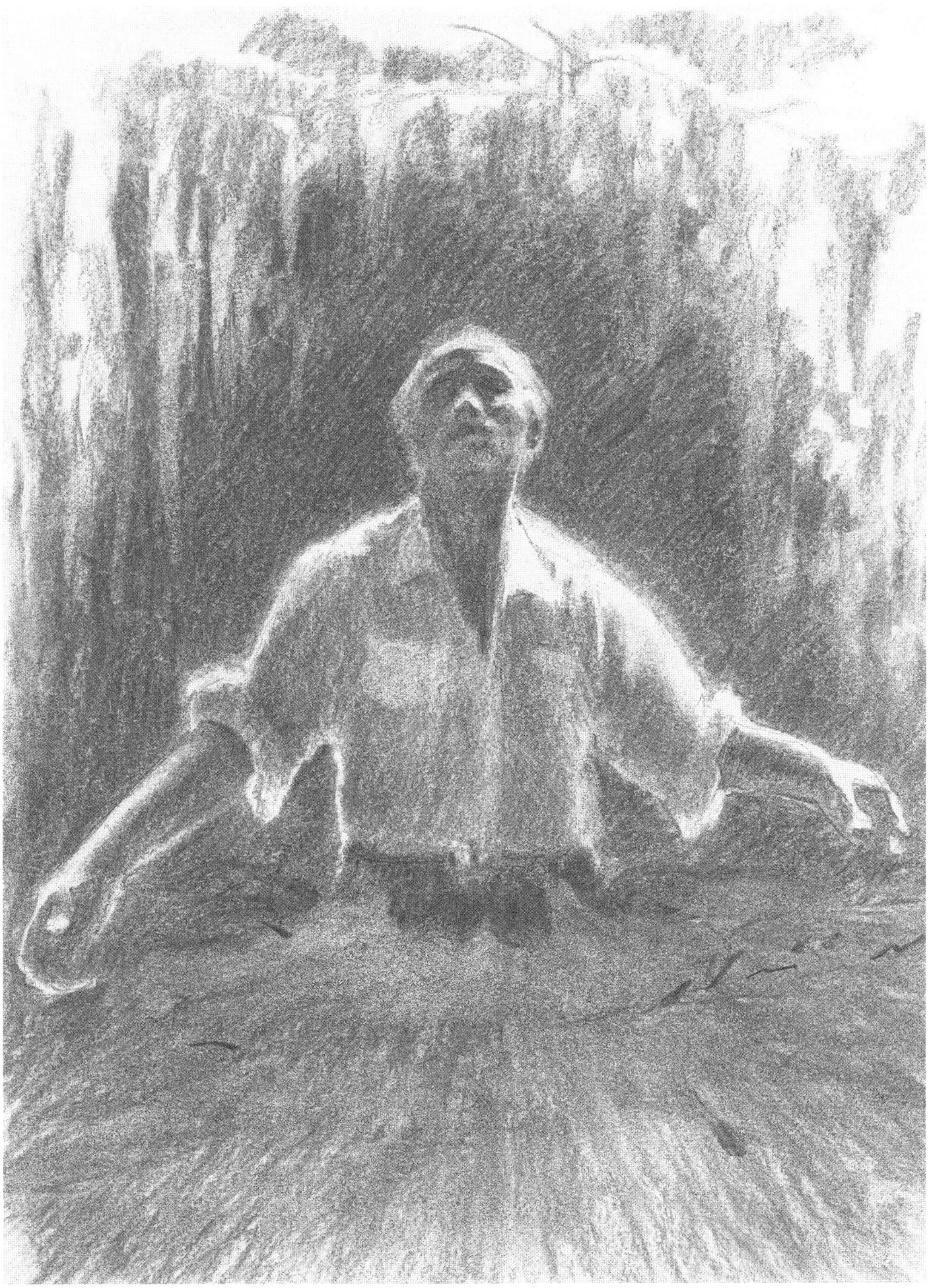

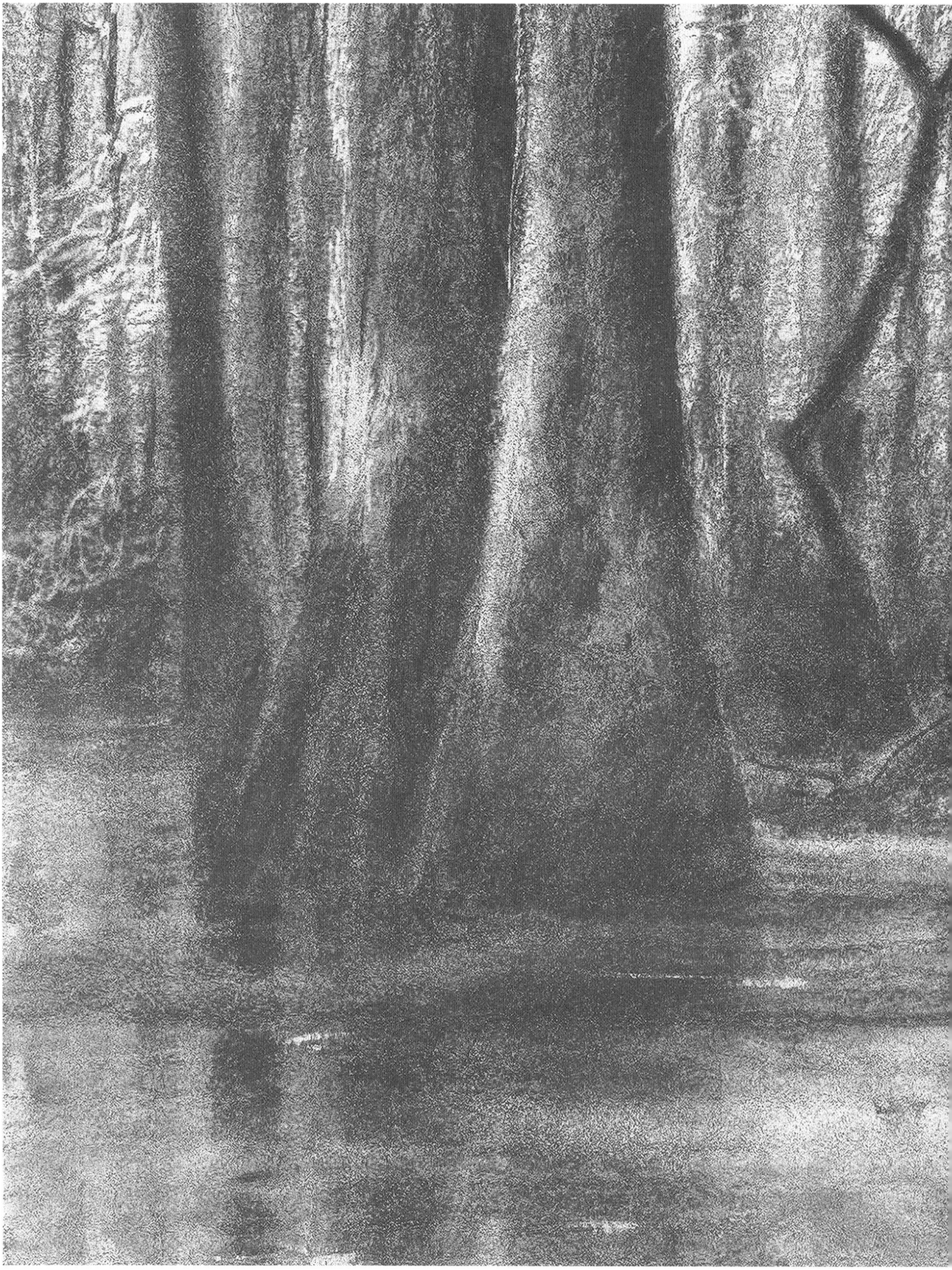

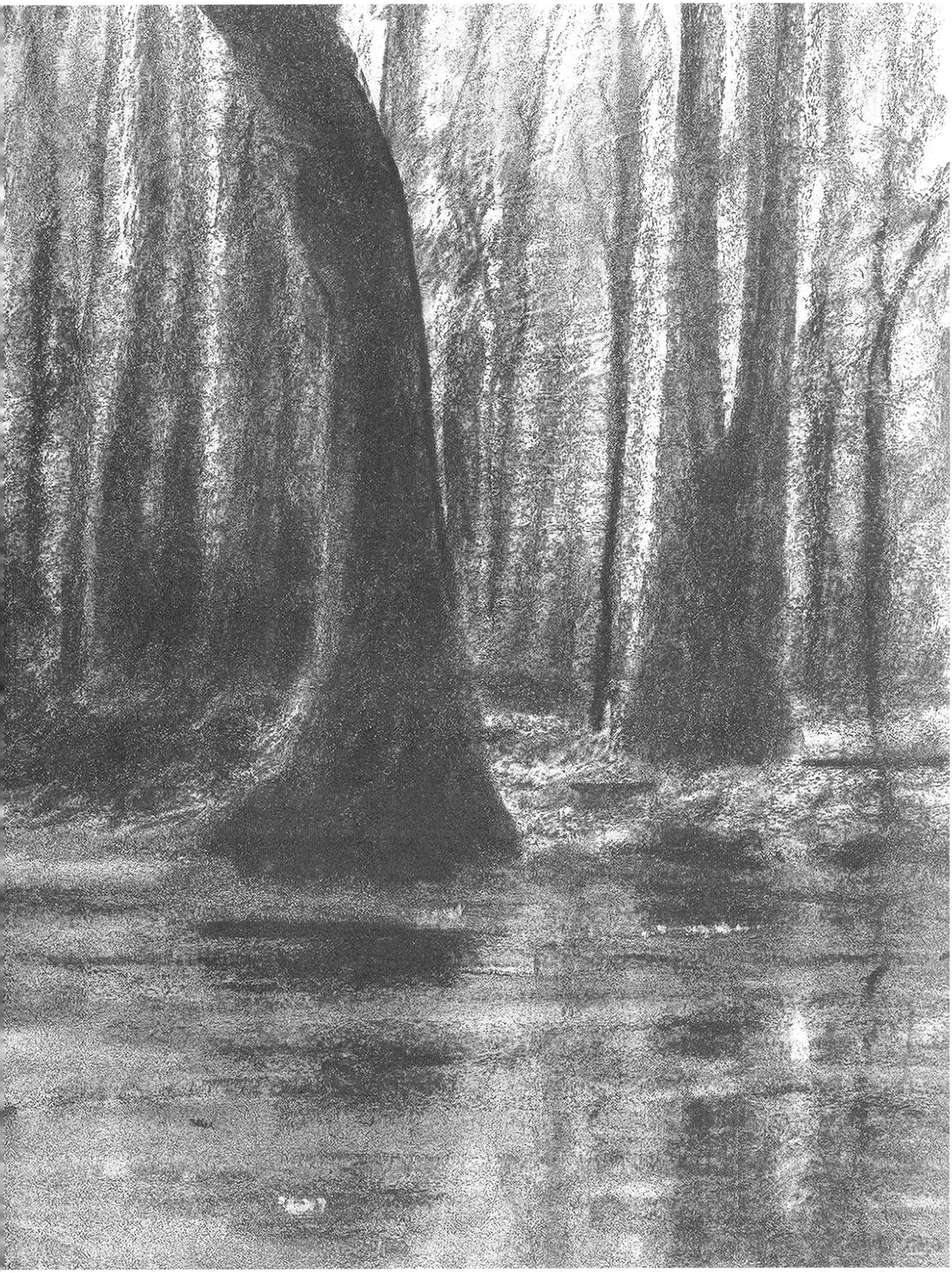

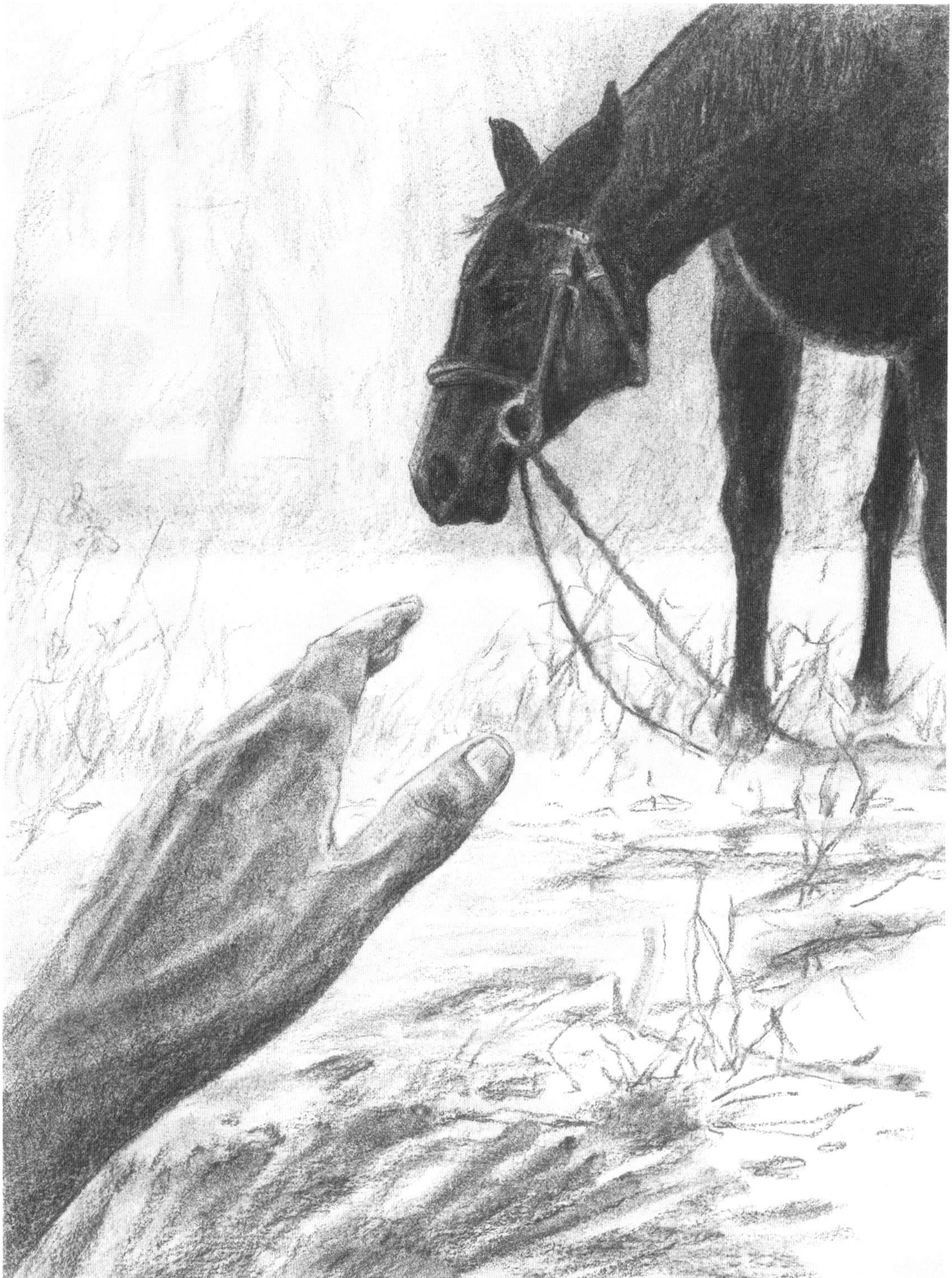

Those who have had hairbreadth escapes from great danger can seldom describe their experiences calmly, if they describe them truly. And when I think of the dread grip of that black hole, even now I cannot suppress a shudder and a sickness at heart. I remember at that moment, as if looking on them for the last time, how blue and sweet was the sky, tinged with the sunset's gold; how misty and still the woods, how beautiful the wide world from whose vision I was being brutally dragged.

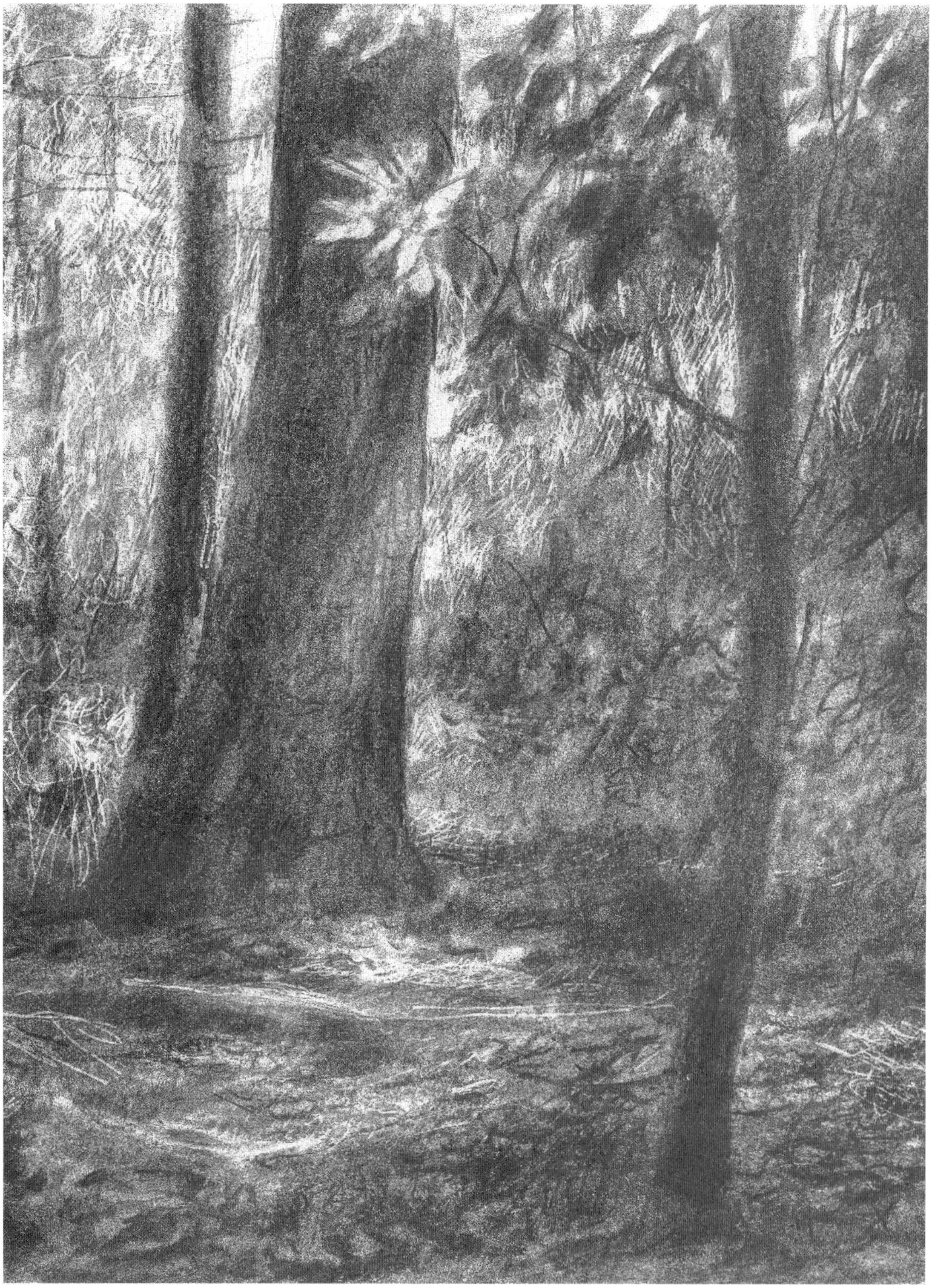

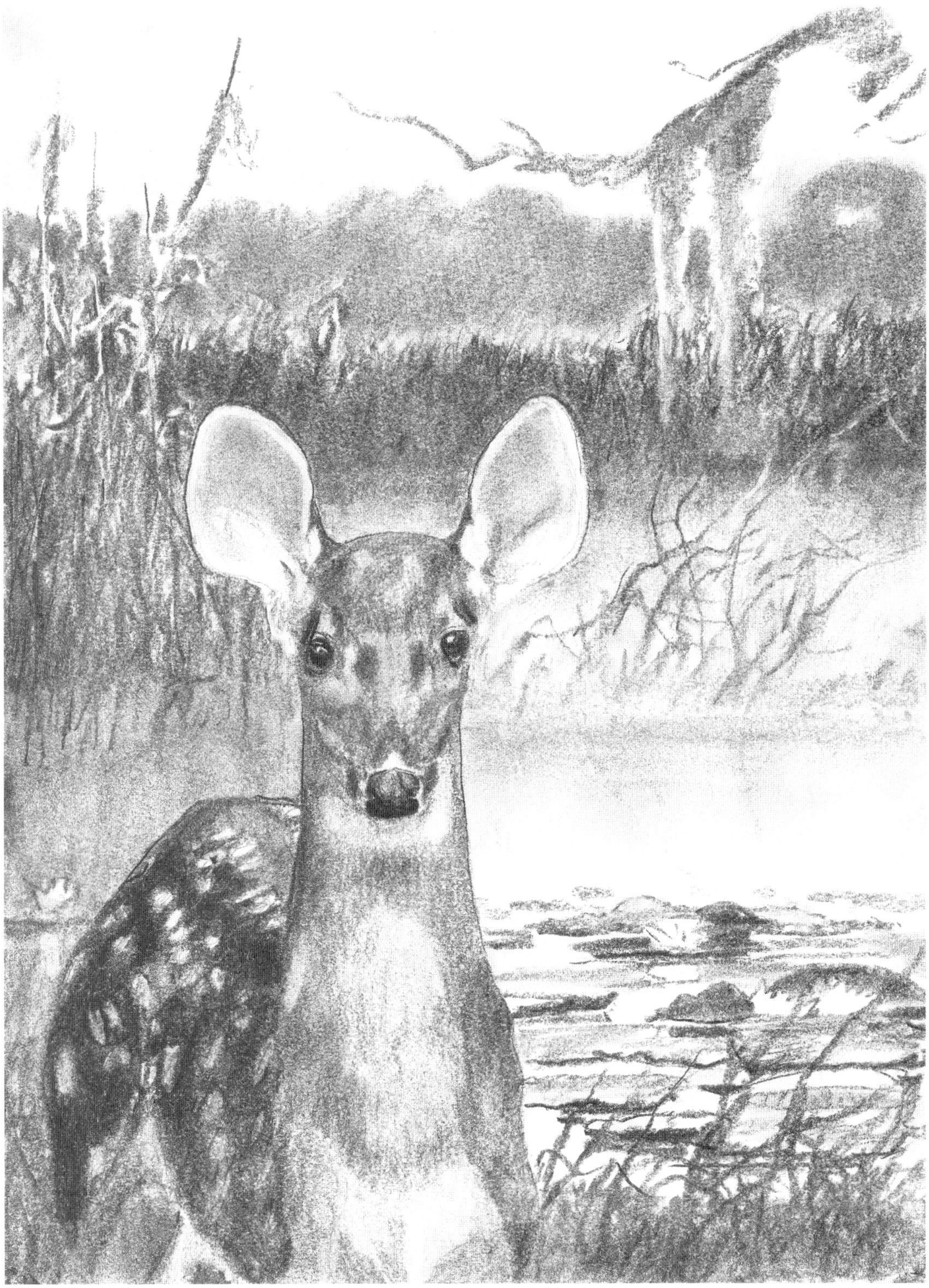

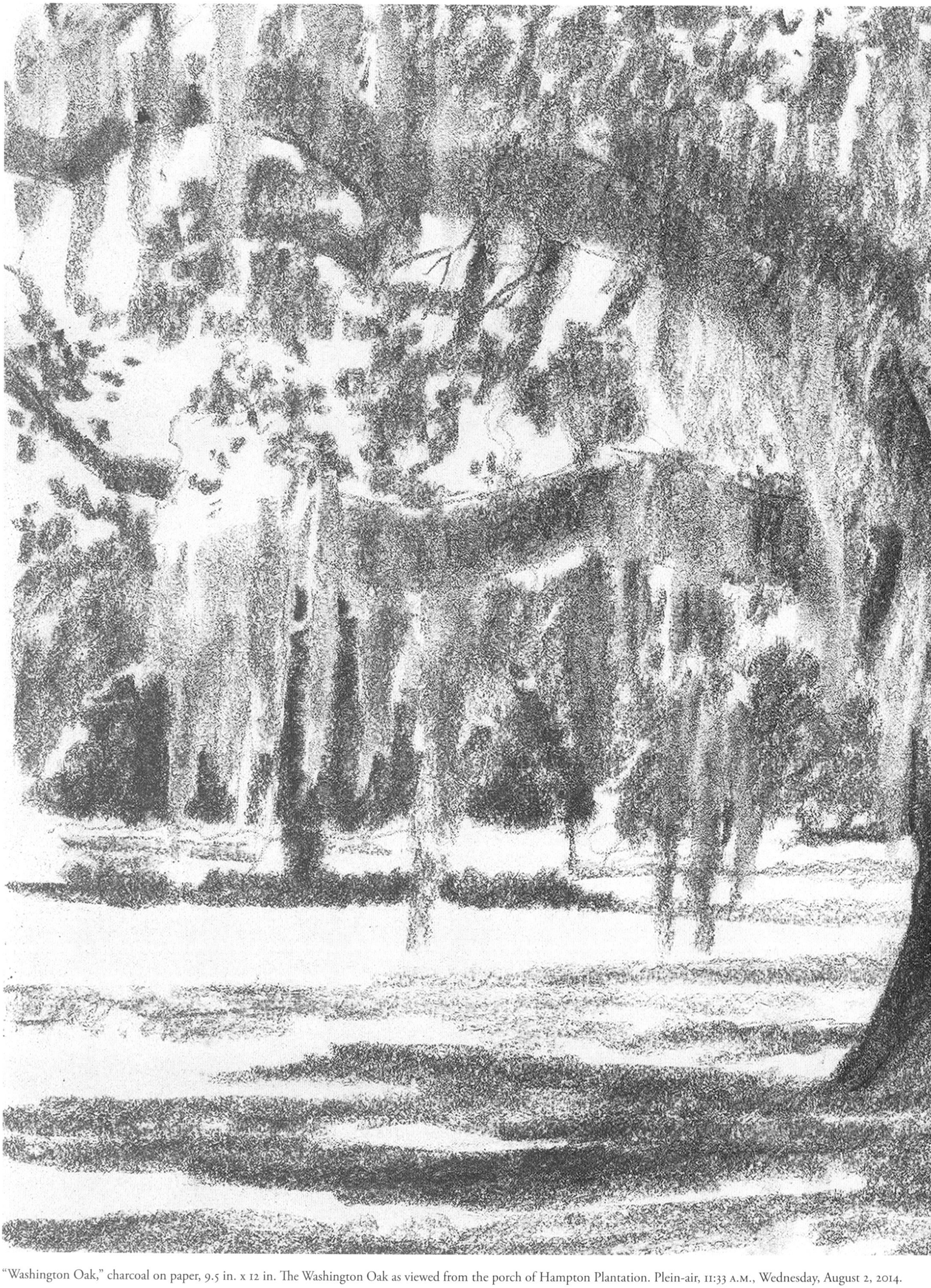

"Washington Oak," charcoal on paper, 9.5 in. x 12 in. The Washington Oak as viewed from the porch of Hampton Plantation. Plein-air, 11:33 A.M., Wednesday, August 2, 2014.

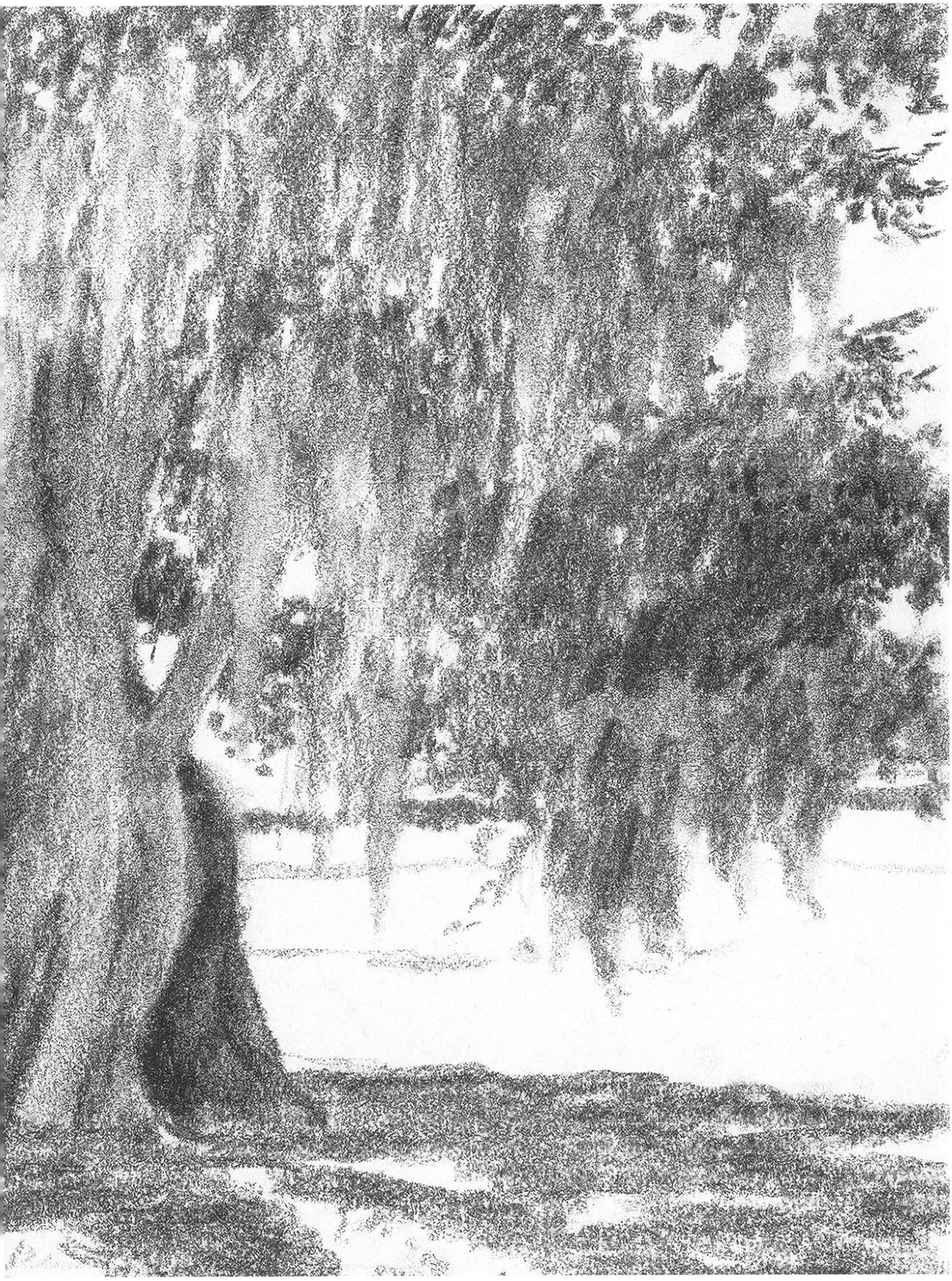

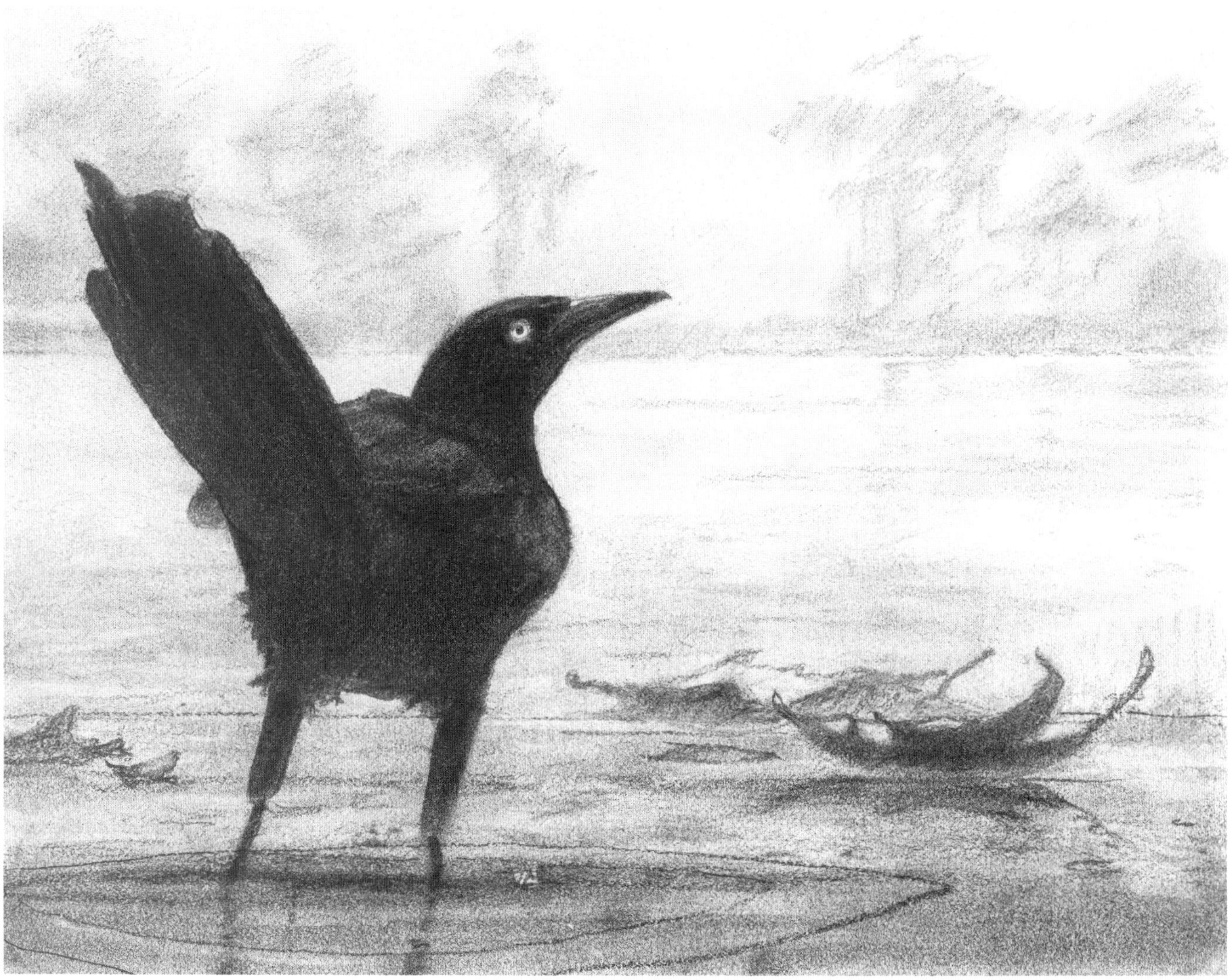

Savagely risking the peril of the effort, I grasped a handful of the fatal blue flags, wrenched them off, and held them with desperate entreaty toward the faithful Redbird. He took a step toward me, then another. The sands already had him round the fetlocks, yet he came on, his head outstretched toward the flowers, and the precious bridle dangling low. He felt the undertow, and he walked gingerly. Yet now he reached his head out far, far. I too strained forward, both hands clutching the flowers. Was he close enough? If I frightened him, he would bound away. I prayed.

My efforts of reaching forward had caused the sands to drag me heavily downward. They closed over my shoulders. They flowed about my throat, fondling it coldly. With a last despairing cry I threw out my arms, and my hands gripped the reins with a grip of death. My fingers were steel bands. My breath was all but gone. My strength seemed pressed up into my arms.

Redbird threw up his head, snorting, backing, plunging. He racked and tore my shoulders cruelly. Then he lay back on the bridle, and I grew sick over the mortal strain. He sank in the sands; his powerful neck arched, and his shapely breast muscles ripped and swelled. And out of the pit I came, out of the horrible morass he drew me out on the hard white sands, out on the friendly green grass, out into the wide, sweet world again, Redbird, my Redbird!

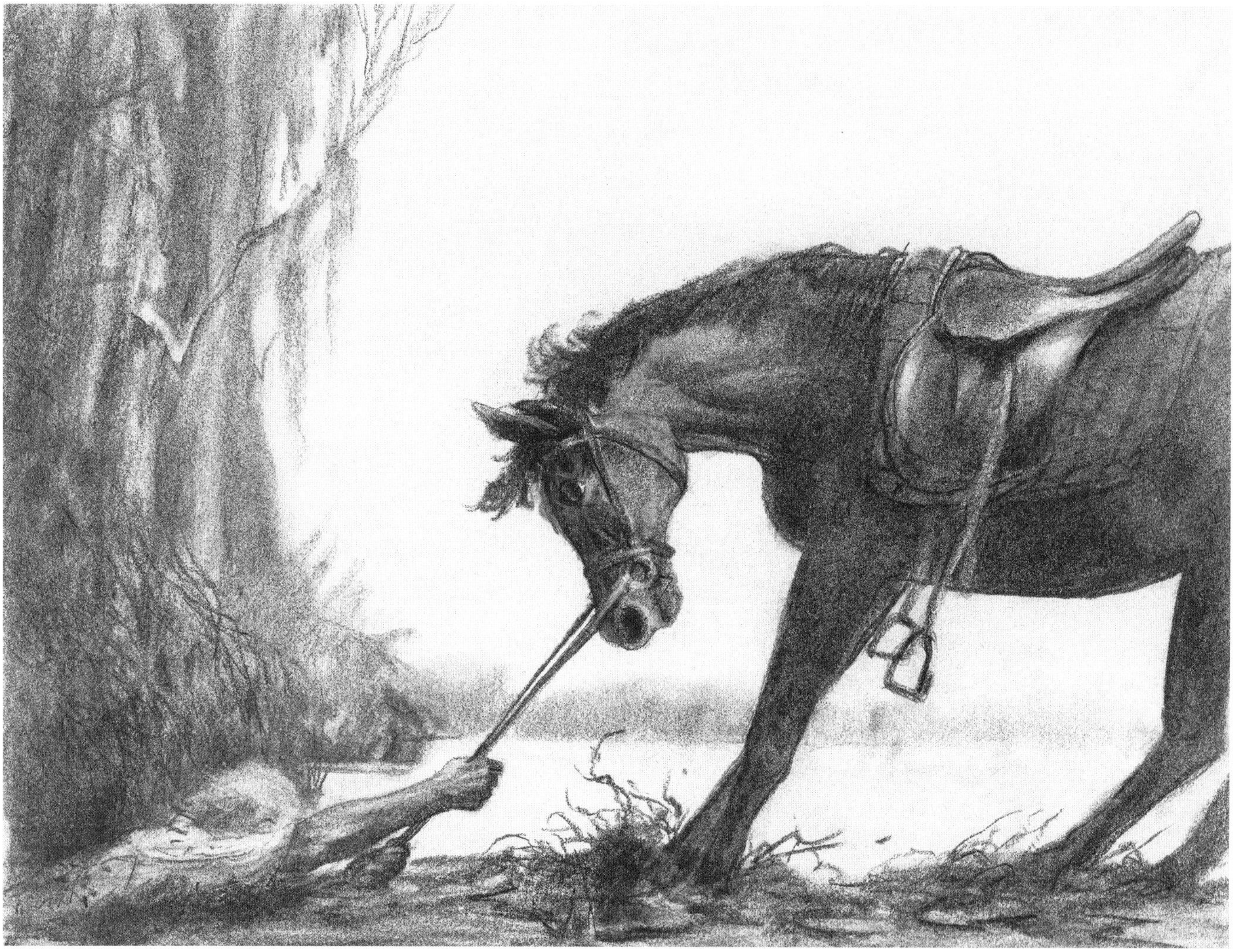

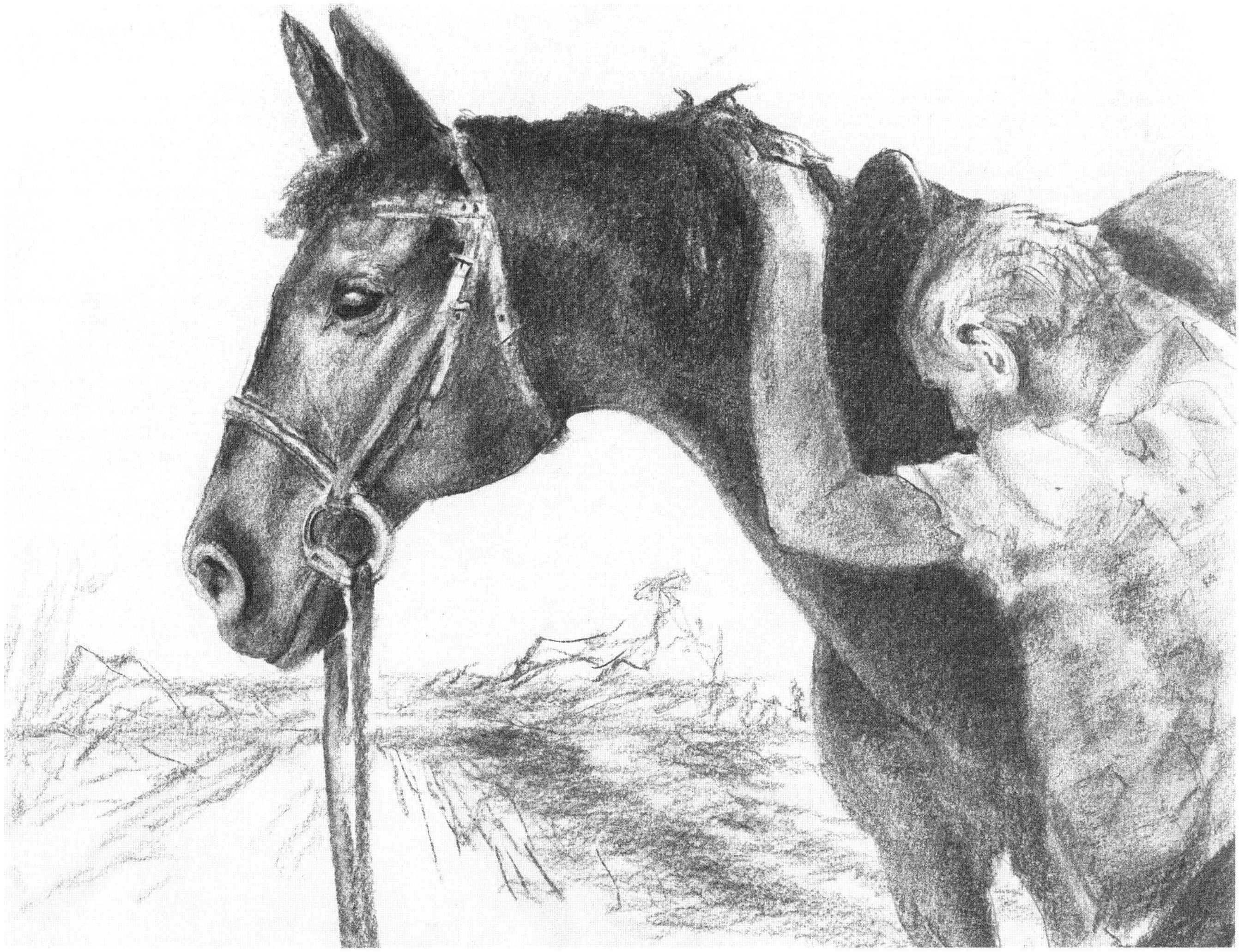

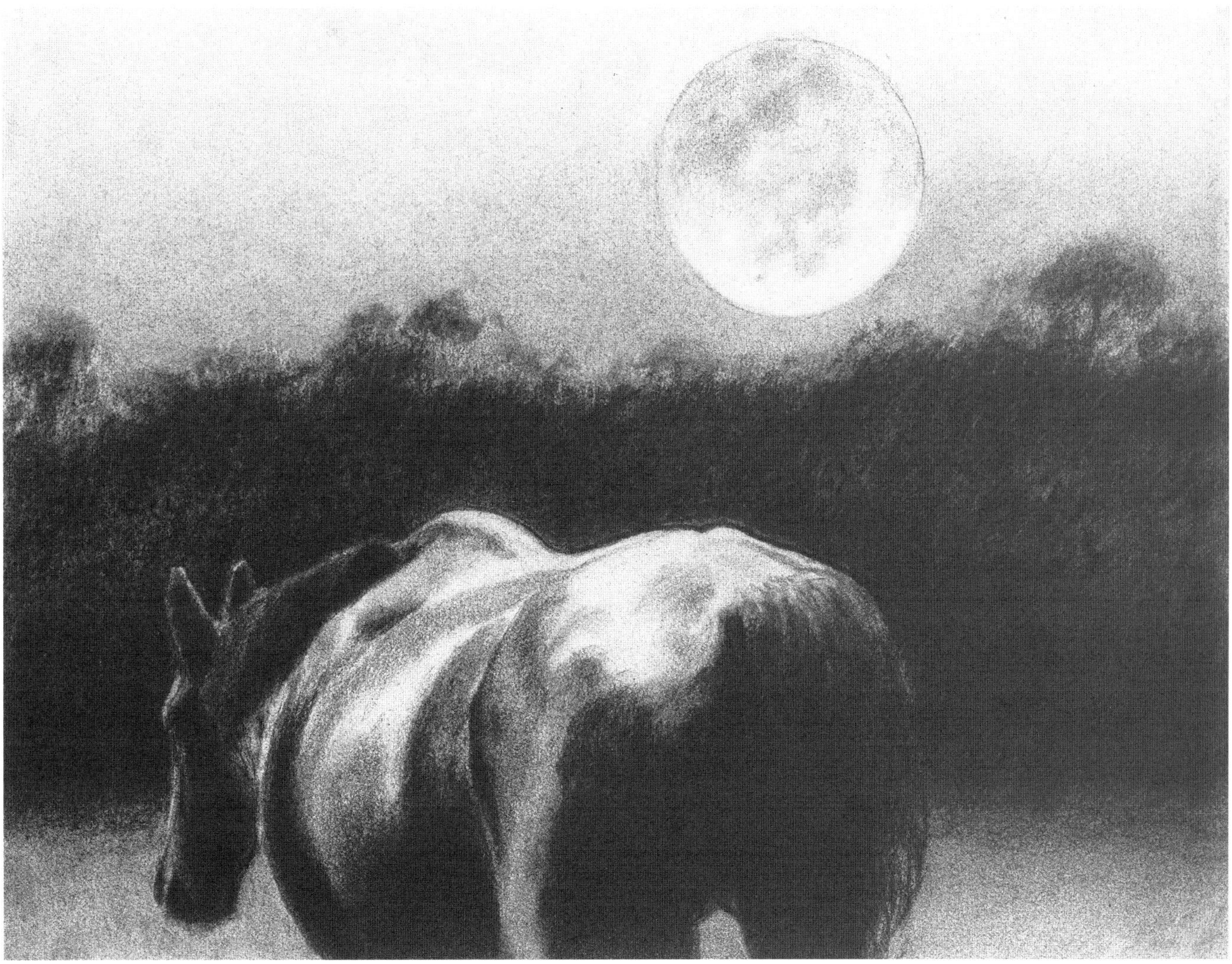

Afterword

Charles W. Waring III

Naturalists and sportsmen keenly appreciate the verisimilitude a writer must employ to take readers to a cherished spot—some place etched in one's memory. This is the hallowed ground where the author and reader have both encountered the splendor of man meeting nature in a spectacular manner. In such a spirit of tapping into lowcountry living more than a century ago, the modern reader should imagine that "The Doom of Ravenswood" might have originated by the fireside at Hampton Plantation one chilly evening as Archibald Rutledge prepared his children for bed, stoking their imaginations and filling them with courage and faith. Longtime fans of Bard Rutledge may read this story and also recall his famous essay about the importance of educating one's children about the pure joy to be found in outdoor experiences, particularly hunting.

In his timeless "Why I Brought My Boys Up to Be Hunters," Mr. Rutledge gives parents an essential and humor-packed lesson in raising their youngsters in the face of ubiquitous materialism and urban pastimes. He writes, "And it is my fixed conviction that if a parent can give his children a passionate and wholesome devotion to the outdoors, the fact that he cannot leave each of them a fortune does not really matter so much." The author, in this essay first published in *Field and Stream* in 1932, also makes an impassioned promise that woods-wise little ones will "worship the Creator in his mighty works."

Packed tightly into his *Life's Extras* from 1928, Bard Rutledge speaks to the enjoyment of such beauty as the "manifestation of divine art." His son, Irvine, wrote an introduction to a 1983 reprint of this slim volume, which has been a success to several publishers who have collectively sold more than one million copies. Judge Rutledge said: "This little book represents my father at his best and illustrates his love of nature, his deep faith, and his spiritual vision." The substantial *Deep River* collection of poems provides a cathedral full of spiritual verses for those seeking further affirmation of the foundations and perspective of this favorite son of the literary lowcountry.

Hence, it should not surprise readers to find Christian images throughout "The Doom of Ravenswood"; the protagonist even explicitly states that he prayed for his horse to pull him from the quicksand. The overall struggle in the muck demands a need for someone or something—a Christ-like figure that is his Redbird—to come to his rescue as he faced the "grip of death." Long before

C.S. Lewis wrote *The Chronicles of Narnia* series, Mr. Rutledge addressed the challenge of keeping a child's attention on matters of substance, allowing a dramatic encounter with nature to keep the rhythm of reading alive and offer the opportunity for those Biblical nuances, such as "out of the pit I came."

The desperate horseman speaks to his pride in being strong and knowledgeable about the woods and how such traits did "appear drawbacks" as he struggled in the depths of the swamp. The author telegraphs his view of the tragic nature of self-reliance devoid of a savior when he says: "My fate lay in my own hands; and wretched fate, where to put forth the strength of which I was so proud was but to sink deeper, to strangle, and to die!" The reader is a witness to a drama that tests the horseman's faith in how he might be able to plea to his four-legged companion to get in that exact spot where he can grip the reins and find firmer ground and safety.

Indeed, we have a substantial South Carolina-born allegory to stand up against the stacks of children's books that are little more than cotton candy. In this brief but powerful tale, Mr. Rutledge proves again to be the master of manly, faith-filled messages. He provides an antidote to a modern cultural atmosphere that has all the horror of the quicksand without any of the charm and beauty of the swamp or redemption through the deeds of a noble steed.

In publishing this story and by benefiting the South Carolina Book Festival, the University of South Carolina Press and the state's Humanities Council have honored the heritage that the Palmetto State's first poet laureate provided in a prolific manner. With renowned Rutledge scholar Jim Casada introducing this handsomely illustrated tale, serious followers of "Old Flintlock" are assured of having the authentic experience in the verdant landscape of outdoor literature, one too often riddled with a focus on the consumptive results of sport. Instead, children everywhere may enter a boy's swampy playground that is as real as it is ultimately rewarding.

One may easily imagine Mr. Rutledge's joy-filled face coming to the final sentence and then casting his wee ones over his broad shoulders and carrying them up to bed to rest well before the morning's hunt on his beloved Hampton Plantation. Perhaps, he touted a trot up the staircase or whispered a whinny while tucking in the tots, acting the part of Redbird, exactly the kind of valiant mount required by those who would help him drive the white-tailed deer of the Lowcountry. Bard Rutledge has succeeded again in carrying our thoughts to the countryside where he found life to be especially worth living, giving his Creator the opportunity to test his faith while showcasing the blessings of the beauty that lingers in the minds of those who make time to meet nature on her own terms.

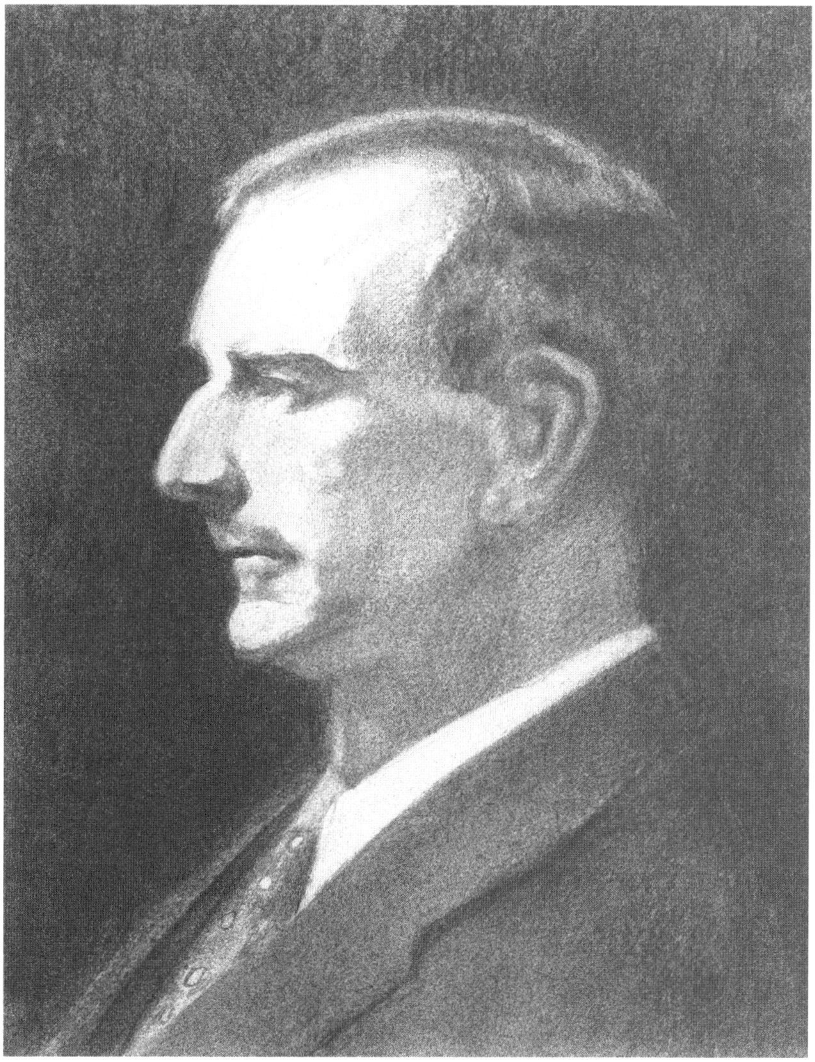

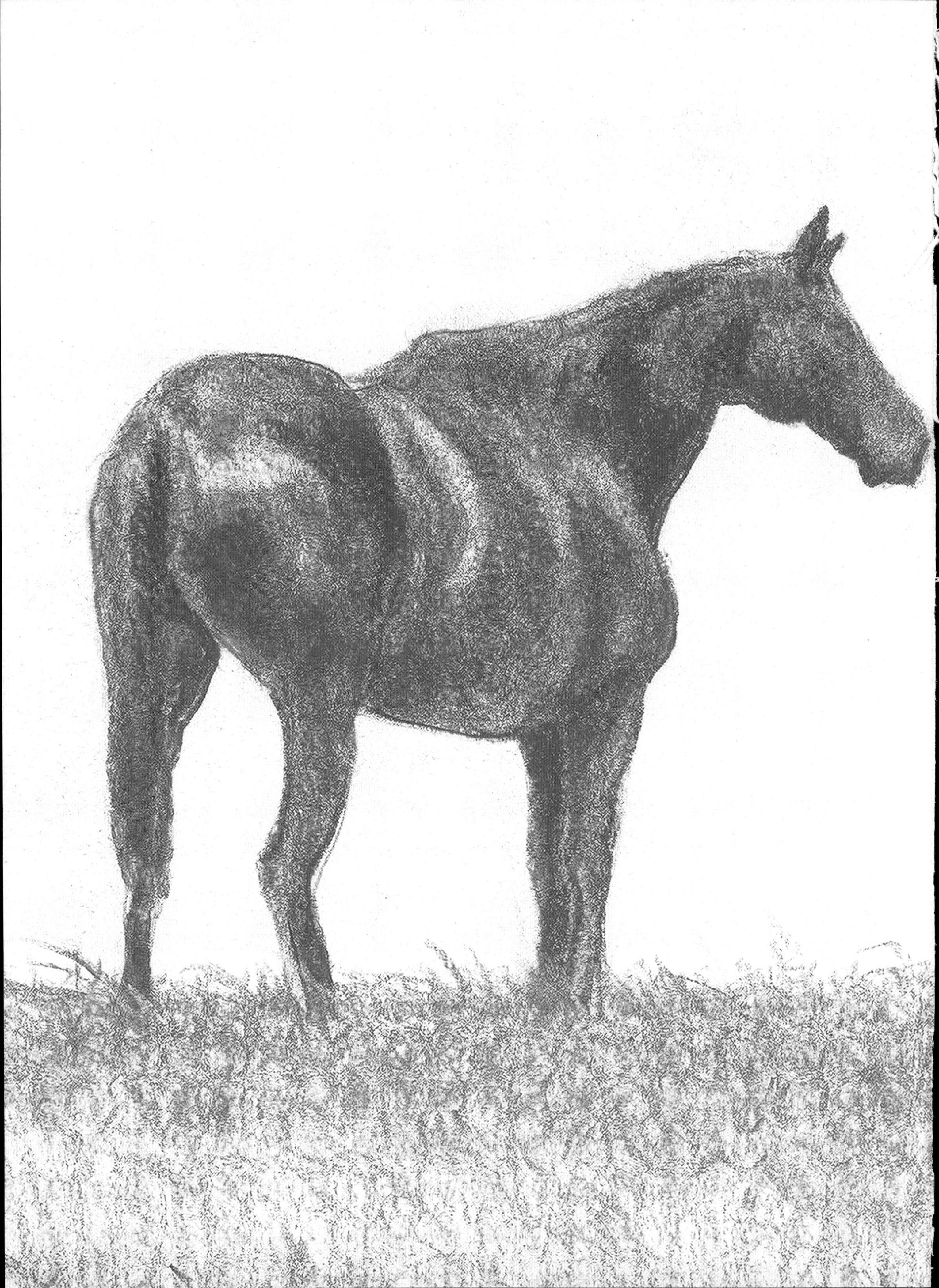